"Good book?"

A deep, velvety voice ~~penetrated~~ the cold, swirling mists of the Yorkshire moors, jerking Ellie back into the twenty-first century.

Being startled while perched on top of a ladder was always going to be risky. If she'd been the waiflike heroine of one of those top-shelf romances, Ellie would at this point have dropped tidily into his arms, and the fool, having taken one look, would have fallen instantly and madly in love with her.

Since this was reality, and she was built on rather more substantial lines than the average heroine of a romance—who wasn't?—she fell on him like the proverbial ton of bricks, and they went down in a heap of tangled limbs....

*Harlequin Romance® is thrilled to present
another wonderful book from
multi-award-winning author*

Liz Fielding

*Liz Fielding will keep you captivated
for hours with her contemporary,
witty and feel-good romances....*

Praise for her RITA® Award-winning novels!

The Best Man and the Bridesmaid
Winner of the RITA® Award
for 2001 Traditional Category

"...a delightful tale with a fresh spin on a fan-favorite
storyline, snappy dialogue and charming characters."
—*Romantic Times BOOKreviews*

The Marriage Miracle
Winner of the RITA® Award for 2006 Best Short
Contemporary Romance

"...a charming combination of reality and fantasy,
liberally laced with humor. Truly excellent."
—*Romantic Times BOOKreviews*

LIZ FIELDING

The Secret Life of Lady Gabriella

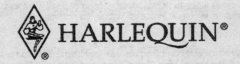

HARLEQUIN®

TORONTO • NEW YORK • LONDON
AMSTERDAM • PARIS • SYDNEY • HAMBURG
STOCKHOLM • ATHENS • TOKYO • MILAN • MADRID
PRAGUE • WARSAW • BUDAPEST • AUCKLAND

ISBN-13: 978-0-373-03951-7
ISBN-10:   0-373-03951-4

THE SECRET LIFE OF LADY GABRIELLA

First North American Publication 2007.

Copyright © 2007 by Liz Fielding.

www.eHarlequin.com

Printed in U.S.A.

Liz Fielding was born with itchy feet. She made it to Zambia before her twenty-first birthday and, gathering her own special hero and a couple of children on the way, lived in Botswana, Kenya and Bahrain—with pauses for sightseeing pretty much everywhere in between. She finally came to a full stop in a tiny Welsh village cradled by misty hills, and these days mostly leaves her pen to do the traveling. When she's not sorting out the lives and loves of her characters, she potters in the garden, reads her favorite authors and spends a lot of time wondering, What if…? For news of upcoming books—and to sign up for her occasional newsletter—visit Liz's Web site at www.lizfielding.com.

Books

HARLEQUIN ROMANCE
THE FIVE-YEAR BABY SECRET
THE SHEIKH'S GUARDED HEART
THE VALENTINE BRIDE

This book is dedicated to every woman
who ever picked up a duster or fell off a stepladder.
Especially if she fell on the man of her dreams.

CHAPTER ONE

'LADY MARCH?'

Ellie's tongue was glued to the roof of her mouth. This was such a mistake. She wasn't a 'lady'. She shouldn't be here. She should own up right now...

'I apologise for keeping you waiting,' Jennifer Cochrane continued, 'but there was a crisis at the printers I had to deal with.'

Unable to speak, Ellie attempted an answering smile. Even in her borrowed clothes, hair swirled up in a sophisticated style and wearing more make-up than she'd normally wear in a month, she'd been expecting someone to point a finger at her, shout 'impostor' the moment she'd stepped within the hushed portals of the offices of *Milady* magazine.

She'd never meant to take it this far.

Never expected to get this far.

Wouldn't be here if the idea of her contributing saleable copy to a magazine aimed directly at ladies who, in between chauffeuring their offspring about in top-of-the-range 4x4s, lunched, gossiped and shopped hadn't produced such howls of mirth at her writers' group.

She'd set out to show them—show herself, maybe—

that while she might miss the magazine's target audience by a mile, she was professional enough to write whatever was required.

And she'd done it.

She'd read a dozen or so back copies of the magazine, looked for a gap that she could fill, and 'Lady Gabriella's Journal' had been the result.

Written in the crisp, upper-class style of the magazine, she'd offered the jottings of the 'perfect' reader. Highlights in the life of a woman with three children, several well-bred and perfectly behaved dogs, and all the time in the world to devote to interior design, her garden, entertaining and sitting on worthy committees. 'Lady Gabriella' was, of course, married to a man with the means to pay for it all.

She'd actually enjoyed writing it, vicariously living a completely different life if only on paper. Having no trouble at all imagining herself the 'lady of the house' rather than simply caretaking the place during the owner's absence.

Then, since she'd done the work, she'd submitted it to the magazine, enclosing some of her doodly drawings as an afterthought—an impression of the gothic turret that adorned one end of the house, the cat sitting in the deep embrasure of an arched window, a toddler (Lady G's youngest)—expecting a swift thanks-but-no-thanks return in the self-addressed envelope provided for the purpose. She'd had enough of them to know the form. But if you didn't try, if you didn't pursue a dream, hunt it down until there was no breath left in your body, let chances slip by, then what was the point?

The letter, addressed to Lady Gabriella March, inviting her for a 'chat', should have been enough. She would show it to the writers' group and take a bow, point proved. Except it wasn't.

This was a never-to-be-repeated chance to talk to the editor of a famous, if fading, magazine—which was why she was here, in the office of Jennifer Cochrane, a woman of advanced years but formidable character, who had the style, diction and classic wardrobe—including the mandatory double row of pearls—of one of the minor royals. One of the seriously scary ones.

Transformed by her disapproving sister, Stacey, into Lady Gabriella March for the day, it took all her concentration to put down the cup she was holding without spilling the contents over the designer suit that Stacey—another formidable woman—had lent her for the occasion. To then stand up and cross the inches-deep carpet in precariously high heels—also her sister's—without falling flat on her face.

Having left it too late to cut and run, she had no choice but follow through. Breathe... Concentrate, she told herself. One foot in front of the other, the walk functional rather than flirty. Sedate duchess rather than saucy domestic...

Having managed to negotiate the coffee cup and carpet without disaster, she offered her hand and said, 'How d'you do, Mrs Cochrane?'

She was convinced she looked, and sounded, exactly like Eliza Doolittle at Ascot—just before she let slip the expletive...

Mrs Cochrane, however, appeared to notice nothing amiss in this performance, and offered her an unexpectedly warm smile, waving her away from the desk towards the more informal sofa.

'We're both busy women, Lady March, so I'm not

going to waste time. I enjoyed the diary pieces you sent me. And the drawings you used to illustrate them.'

'Really?' Oh, that wasn't cool. But she'd never been face to face with an editor before, let alone had a 'chat' with one. She tried to restrain the idiotic grin, slow the heart-rate to something more stately. 'Thank you.'

'The drawings have a delightful spontaneity, as if you'd just doodled your thoughts.'

'Oh, I did,' she exclaimed, then inwardly groaned as Mrs Cochrane smiled. This was definitely not the way to do it… Then, in an effort to recover the situation, 'I did plan to go to art school…'

Which was true. But common sense ran like a seam of iron ore through her family genes, and she'd seen the value of a good solid degree and a teaching qualification. Something practical that she could use all her life. Would fit around married life, children.

She shrugged—then wondered if a 'Lady', one with a capital L, would shrug—and left Mrs Cochrane to draw her own conclusions.

'Clearly you chose marriage and children instead,' Mrs Cochrane filled in for her, nodding and smiling with obvious approval. 'Most young women seem to be leaving it so late these days.'

Fortunately she was looking at the drawings, spread across the low table in front of them, giving Ellie a moment to recover.

She picked one that was no more than a few lines suggesting the upraised bottom, the chubby legs of an infant almost ready to stand up and take her first steps.

'This is Chloe? Your youngest child?'

Ellie looked at the picture. It was the daughter of one

of the women she worked for in her 'day' job, drawn from memory without a thought.

How could she have done that?

'Charming,' Mrs Cochrane said, without waiting for an answer. Then, 'I'm going to be frank with you, Lady March—'

'Gabriella, please.'

'Gabriella. I've been looking for someone who can write a regular lifestyle column for some time. It has been extraordinarily difficult to find a writer capable of finding just the tone our readers appreciate.'

Ellie was not entirely surprised to hear that; no one born since 1950 wrote that way.

'There was always just a suggestion of the pastiche. A lack of sincerity.' She smiled. 'Sincerity is essential.'

'Absolutely,' she managed, wishing the floor would open up and swallow her. Right now.

'Of course I'm not interested in the rather dated diary format.'

Which was the sole reason she'd chosen it. And, from a point where she had been praying to whatever saint was supposed to be looking after the interests of neophyte writers to get on with sorting out that hole for her to disappear into, she was suddenly indignant. Why bring her all the way up to London for a 'chat' about her work, then tell her that it wasn't what was wanted?

'I'm looking for something less formal—something that will appeal to the younger generation of women we need to attract. Your writing has a lively freshness, a touch of irreverence that is quite striking.'

All the things she'd done her absolute best to suppress...

'What I'd like to suggest to you is a regular contribution based on your own experiences of entertaining, household management, the small oddities of family life. Not a diary as such, more a conversation with the reader. A chat over coffee, or lunch with a friend.'

Everything about that sounded perfect—if she ignored the fact that she didn't have a partner, let alone a husband and the charmingly precocious children she'd invented were an amalgam of those she'd encountered in her 'day' job—or at least their mothers' sadly mistaken assessment of them. As for entertaining, the only effort she put into that was to call out for a pizza.

And what the heck was 'household management' when it was at home?

'My proposal is this. An initial contract for six months at our usual rate, and then, if the readers respond as favourably as I anticipate, we'll talk again. Does that interest you?'

This, Ellie decided, was about as close to her worst nightmare as it was possible to get. She'd finally got her first breakthrough, her first real recognition as a writer, and it was all based on lies.

She couldn't do it.

'I expect you'd like a little time to consider it?' Mrs Cochrane said, when she didn't immediately answer.

Could she?

'Maybe you'd like to talk it over with your husband?' she pressed.

'My husband?' To hear the words, spoken so casually, left her momentarily floundering. 'No,' she finally managed. 'That won't be necessary.'

Sean, wherever he was, would be grinning like an idiot, cheering her on, saying, 'You show them, Ellie. Take the balloon ride…'

Mrs Cochrane really liked what she'd written. She'd be doing the woman a favour if she said yes. And she'd be getting paid for writing on a regular basis—proof for her parents, her sister, that she wasn't just chasing some will-o'-the-wisp daydream. She'd have something to show an agent, too. And she'd only be writing under a pseudonym of sorts, after all. People did that all the time.

Actually, maybe she wouldn't even have to do that...

'Perhaps,' she suggested, 'younger readers would be put off by the title? Maybe I should just write as Gabriella March?'

Please, please, please...

The other woman considered her suggestion for all of ten seconds before she shook her head. 'Lady Gabriella has a touch of class.' Then, 'Is it your husband's title, or a courtesy one?'

'A courtesy one,' she said, seizing on this. If it was just a courtesy title, it wouldn't mean anything. Except that Mrs Cochrane was looking at her as if she expected more, and Ellie suddenly had the feeling that she'd just made a huge mistake, somehow given the wrong answer. But it was too late now, and having made the mental leap from 'no way can I do this' to 'what's the problem?' she tuned out the voice of sanity.

Chances like this were once-in-a-lifetime opportunities, and no one knew better than she did that they had to be grabbed with both hands.

She'd worry about the children and the household management later. There were books. The internet...

As for her 'husband'...

For a moment Ellie was assailed by such an ache of loneliness, loss. How could she do this...? Pretend...

'Well, to business,' Mrs Cochrane said, when it was

clear she wasn't going to add anything on the subject of
her 'title', and by the time she'd explained the techni-
calities of a monthly column, the needs of word count,
copy dates, etc, Ellie had recovered.

'We'd like you to send two or three illustrations with
each month's column. Can you manage that?'

Illustrations were the least of her problems. She drew
as she breathed—always had done—without even
thinking about it.

'We may not use them all, but it will give the art director
a choice. Those will be paid for separately, of course.'

They would?

'In fact, for your masthead, rather than a photograph
of you, I'd like to use this drawing of your house.'

Her house.

That would be one she was house-sitting, for an
absent aging academic who was studying some long-
lost language in foreign parts.

'That's not a problem for you? Clearly you'll want
to keep a measure of privacy?'

'No,' she said. A problem would have been if Mrs
Cochrane had wanted a photograph of her. That would
have blown her cover on day one, and she doubted Mrs
Cochrane would be amused to discover that Lady
Gabriella, far from being a lady of leisure, was Ellie
March, a very hardworking cleaning lady.

Her drawing, on the other hand, was no more than
an impression. The turret, a window or two, a terrace.
It could be anywhere.

'I think that's a great idea.'

'Well?' Stacey demanded, when she returned her suit
and shoes. 'What did she want?'

'To offer me a contract to write a monthly lifestyle column for the magazine.'

Ellie took great satisfaction in watching her clever, successful older sister's jaw drop.

It didn't take her long to recover.

'You're pulling my leg, aren't you?' Then, perhaps realising that was a little harsh, 'I mean, it's ridiculous. You don't have a lifestyle. Let's face it, you don't even have a life.'

'True,' Ellie said, keeping her face straight with the greatest difficulty. 'But you're missing the point. I write fiction. I'll make it up.'

'Good book?'

A deep, velvety voice penetrated the cold, swirling mists of the Yorkshire Moors, jerking Ellie back into the twenty-first century.

Not an entirely bad thing.

She'd started the afternoon with the intention of giving the study a thorough bottoming. Keeping on top of the dust in the rambling old house she was 'sitting' while its owner was away was not onerous, but it did require a schedule or she lost track; today it was the study's turn. Unfortunately, her attention had been grabbed by the unexpected discovery of a top-shelf cache of gothic romances, and she'd forgotten all about the dust.

But, then again, it was not entirely good, either.

Being startled while perched on top of a ladder was always going be risky. On a library ladder with an inclination to take off on its tracks at the slightest provocation, it was just asking for trouble. And trouble was what Ellie got.

Twice.

Losing her balance six feet above ground was bad enough, but her attempt to recover it proved disastrous as the ladder shifted sideways, taking her feet with it.

Too busy attempting to defy the laws of gravity to yell at the fool who'd caused the problem, she dropped her duster and made a desperate grab for the bookshelf with one hand—while clinging tightly to the precious leather-bound volume she'd been reading in the other.

For a moment, as her fingertips made contact with the shelf, she thought it was going to be all right.

She quickly discovered that she'd been over-optimistic, and that in lunging for the shelf—the laws of physics being what they were—she'd only made things worse.

. Her body went one way; her feet went the other.

Fingers and shelf parted company.

Happily—or not, depending upon your point of view—the author of her misfortune took the full force of her fall.

If she'd been the waif-like heroine of one of those top-shelf romances—or indeed of her own growing pile of unpublished manuscripts—Ellie would, at this point, have dropped tidily into his arms and the fool, having taken one look, would have fallen instantly and madly in love with her. Of course there would have to be several hundred pages of misunderstandings and confusion before he finally admitted it, either to himself or to her, since men tended to be a bit dense when it came to romance.

Since this was reality, and she was built on rather more substantial lines than the average heroine of a romance—who wasn't?—she fell on him like the proverbial ton of bricks, and they went down in a heap of tangled limbs.

And Emily Brontë gave him a cuff round the ear with her leather binding for good measure.

'Idiot!' she finally managed. But she was winded by her fall, and the word lacked force. Ellie sucked in some air and tried again. 'Idiot!'—much better—'You might have killed me!' Then, because he'd somehow managed to walk through locked doors into a house she was care-taking—as in 'taking care of'—she demanded, 'Who the hell are you, anyway?'

Then, as her brain finally caught up with her mouth—and because burglars rarely stopped to exchange must-read titles with their victims—the answer hit her with almost as much force as she'd landed on him with.

There was only one person he could be.

Dr Benedict Faulkner.

The Dr Benedict Faulkner whose house she was sitting.

The Dr Benedict Faulkner who was supposed to be on the other side of the world, up to his eyes in ancient tribal split infinitives.

The Dr Benedict Faulkner who wasn't due back for another nine months.

Now she had time for a closer look, it was obvious that he was an older incarnation of the lovely youth in a faded black and white photograph on the piano in the drawing room. The one she always gave an extra rub with the duster.

Older, but definitely not 'aging'.

She'd somehow got this picture of him wearing tweeds and glasses, with the stooped and withered shoulders of someone whose life was spent poring over ancient manuscripts.

Not so.

It would seem that he had been either a very late

surprise for his mother, or the offspring of a second, younger wife—because while he was wearing a tweed jacket, that was as far as the cliché went.

The man lying beneath her, it had to be said, could have stepped right out of the pages of one of her own romances. The ones that her own sister insisted on referring to as 'fairy tales for grown-ups'.

She was being condescending—a little unkind, even. Stacey, a high-flying corporate lawyer, was so utterly practical and businesslike that it sometimes seemed impossible that they could be sisters—but Ellie was delighted with the description. Only dull, unimaginative people grew out of fairy tales. Didn't they?

And falling on a man of such hero potential was pure fairy tale—although surely in the fairy tales it didn't hurt quite so much?

Whatever.

Opportunities like this didn't come her way often— make that never—which was why she should be making the most of it. Purely for research purposes. But typically, instead of lying dazed in his arms, her cheek pressed firmly against his accommodating chest, listening to his heart skip a beat as he appreciated the colour of her hair, the softness of her ivory skin, the subtle scent of the lavender furniture polish with which she'd been tending his furniture, she'd berated him like a fishwife.

She groaned and let her head sink back to his chest while she recovered her breath along with her wits.

This was no time to let her wits go wandering. It was a disaster! If he was home, he wouldn't need her to house-sit; she wouldn't have anywhere to live.

Worse.

She wouldn't have his house to fire her imagination on a monthly basis for *Milady*.

Then, realising somewhat belatedly that he hadn't responded to her less than ladylike reaction, or to her demand for identification, she took a closer look at him—no point pretending to swoon; even if he'd been conscious she'd completely messed up the fainting-violet moment—and the swirling confusion of thoughts and impressions coalesced into a single feeling.

Concern.

'Dr Faulkner? Are you okay?'

He didn't look okay.

His eyes were closed and he looked somewhat yellow. As if his colour had drained away under a light tan.

She knew she hadn't killed him. Under her hand—which had somehow found its way inside his jacket, to lie flat against his chest—his heartbeat was as steady as a rock. It was, however, entirely possible that she, or more likely Emily's solid leather-bound spine, had knocked him out cold.

'Dr Faulkner?'

His mouth moved, which was encouraging, but no sound emerged. Which was not.

Fully prepared, despite her own close call—and a growing awareness of pain in various bits of her body—to leap heroically into Florence Nightingale mode, Ellie lifted her head to take a better look.

'Where does it hurt?'

His response was little more than a grunt.

'I'm sorry. I didn't catch that.'

'I said,' he repeated, eyes still closed, teeth tightly gritted, 'that you don't want to know.'

She frowned.

'Just move your damned knee…'

'What?' Ellie leaned back, provoking a very audible gasp of pain. Belatedly realising exactly where her knee was lodged, she swiftly lifted herself clear, provoking another grunt as she levered herself up off his chest with her hands. 'Sorry,' she muttered. 'But it was that or the…' She managed to stop her runaway mouth before it reminded him about the knee.

Obviously at this point any fictional heroine worth her salt would have picked up her injured hero's hand and held it clasped against her bosom as she stroked back the lick of dark honey-coloured hair that had tumbled over his high brow. Or maybe administered the kiss of life…

Confronted by reality, Ellie didn't need telling that none of the above would be either appropriate or welcome, and so she confined herself to a brisk, 'Is there anything I can do?'

The second the words were out of her mouth she regretted them, but Dr Faulkner manfully resisted the opportunity to invite her to kiss it better. Or maybe it was just that he needed all his breath to ease himself into a sitting position. He certainly took his time about it, as if fearing that any injudicious move might prove fatal.

She watched him, ready to leap to his aid should the need arise. It wasn't exactly a strain. Looking at him.

He was—local damage excepted—far from doddery. Or old. On the contrary, Dr Benedict Faulkner's thick, shaggy sun-streaked hair didn't have a single grey hair, and she was prepared to bet that under normal circumstances his pared-to-the-bone features lacked the library pallor of the dedicated academic. As for the exquisitely cut fine tweed jacket he was wearing—and it did look very fine indeed, over a T-shirt and jeans worn soft with use that clung like a second skin to his thighs—it was moulded to a pair of shoulders that would not have been out of place in a rugby scrum, or stroking an oar in the university eight.

And, to go with the great hair and the great body, Dr Faulkner possessed a pair of spectacularly heroic blue eyes. Ellie—again from a purely professional standpoint—considered appropriate adjectives. Periwinkle? No, too girly. Cerulean? Oh, please… Flax? Not bad. Flax had a solid, masculine ring to it—but was it the right blue…?

'What about you?' Dr Faulkner asked, breaking into her thoughts.

'What about me?' Ellie responded, as for the second time that day she was yanked back to reality.

'Who the hell are *you*?'

So, he hadn't been unconscious, then. Just in too much pain to move.

'I'm Gabriella March. I work for your sister. Adele,' she added. Who knew what damage she'd done? 'She asked me to house-sit for you while she was away, since she wouldn't be around to take care of things.'

'House-sit? How long for?'

'Twelve months.'

He responded with a word that suggested he was not noticeably impressed by his sibling's thoughtfulness.

'She expected you to be away for that long.' Then, in case he took that as a criticism, 'I'm sure you had a good reason for coming back early.'

'Will a civil war suffice?' Then, 'If she's away, why didn't she ask you to house-sit for her?'

'Oh, Adele let her flat. Those new places down on

the Quay are snapped up by companies looking for accommodation for senior staff moving into the area. They're so convenient…' Then, because he didn't look especially impressed by the inevitable comparison with his own inconveniently rambling house, she said, 'Since she wouldn't be around to keep an eye on this place and I was having landlord trouble, we did each other a favour.'

'Are you one of her research students?'

'What? Oh, no. I'm her cleaner. And yours, actually,' she said. 'At least I was before I moved in. It's part of the deal now I'm living here. Adele is saving you money.'

'What happened to Mrs Turner?' he asked, apparently not impressed with the fiscal argument.

'Nothing. At least, quite a lot—but nothing bad. She won the Lottery and decided that it was definitely going to change her life.'

'Oh. Right. Well, good for her.'

Could the man be any more restrained?

'Did you hurt yourself?' he asked.

Hurt *herself*? Was he suffering from a memory lapse? Partial amnesia, perhaps? *She* had done nothing. The accident had been entirely his fault…

'When you fell,' he persisted, presumably in case she was too dim to understand. Not that he appeared to care very much. Under the circumstances, she couldn't bring herself to blame him.

'I don't think so.'

'Maybe you should check?' he advised.

'Good idea.' Ellie hauled herself to her feet and discovered that her left knee did hurt quite a bit as she turned. She decided not to mention it. 'How about you?'

Dr Faulkner winced a bit, too, as he finally made it to his feet, and she instinctively put out her hand to help him.

He didn't exactly *flinch*, but it was a close-run thing, and she made a performance of testing her own limbs, flexing a wrist as if she hadn't noticed the way he'd recoiled from her touch.

'Maybe you should take a trip to Casualty?' she suggested. 'Just to be on the safe side.'

'I'll be fine.' Then, 'So where is she? Adele.'

He sounded as if he might have a word or two to say to his sister about inviting someone he didn't know to move into his house.

'She's bug-hunting. In Sarawak. Or was it Senegal? Or it could have been Sumatra...' She shrugged. 'Geography is not my strong point.'

'Bug-hunting?'

Probably not quite precise enough for a philologist, Ellie thought, and, with a little shiver that she couldn't quite contain, said, 'She's hunting for bugs.' Which was quite enough discussion about that subject. 'She's away for six months.' She made a gesture that took in their surroundings. 'She wanted me to make the place look lived in. As a security measure,' she added. 'Turning lights on. Keeping the lawn cut. That sort of thing.'

'And in return you get free accommodation?'

'That's a good deal. Most house-sitters expect not only to be paid, but provided with living expenses, too,' she assured him, while trying out her legs to make sure they were in full working order, since she was going to need them later. The one with the twinge suggested that the evening was not going to be much fun. 'And they don't throw in cleaning for free.'

'No, I'm sure they don't.' Then, having watched her

gyrations and clearly come to the conclusion that she was a lunatic, 'Will you live to dust another shelf, do you think?'

'I appear to be in one piece,' she told him, then gave another little shiver—and this time not because she was thinking of Adele Faulkner and her beloved bugs, or even because she was hoping to gain his sympathy, but at the realisation of how lightly she'd got off. How lightly they'd both got off. 'What on earth did you think you were doing, creeping up on me like that?' she demanded.

'Creeping up on you? Madam, you were so wrapped up in the book you were reading I swear a herd of elephants could have stampeded unnoticed beneath you.'

Madam? *Madam?*

He bent and picked it up, holding it at a little distance, narrowing his eyes as he peered at the spine to see for himself what had held her in such thrall. *'Wuthering Heights?'*

His tone was as withering as any east wind blasting the Yorkshire Moors. Not content with practically killing her, he apparently felt entitled to criticise her taste in literature.

'You can read?' she enquired.

Ellie, rapidly tiring of his attitude, had aimed for polite incredulity. She'd clearly hit the bullseye—with the incredulity, if not the politeness—and as he turned his blue eyes on her she rapidly rethought the colour range.

Steel. Slate...

'If someone helps me with the long words,' he assured her, after the longest pause during which her knee, the good one, buckled slightly.

Then, realising what he'd said, it occurred to her that, despite all evidence to the contrary, he possessed a sense of humour, and she waited for the follow-up smile, fully prepared to forgive him and return it with interest, given the slightest encouragement. She wasn't a woman to hold a grudge.

'But I only bother if there's some point to the exercise.' No smile.

He patted his top pocket. 'Did you notice what happened to my glasses?' he asked, handing her the book.

Ellie was sorely tempted to use it to biff him up the other side of his head, tell him to find his own damn glasses and leave him to it. But she liked living in this house. Actually, no. She *loved* living in this house. Especially when the owner was a long way away, out of the country, doing whatever it was that philologists did on research assignments.

There was something special about buffing up the oak handrail on banisters that had been polished by generations of hands. Cleaning a butler's sink installed not as part of some trendy restoration project but when the house was new, wondering about all the poor women who'd stood in the same spot, up to their elbows in washing soda for a few shillings a week. Sleeping in the little round tower that some upwardly mobile Victorian merchant with delusions of grandeur had added to lend his house a touch of the stately homes.

What a pity Dr Faulkner hadn't stayed wherever he'd been. Because, while his sister had been totally happy with the mutual benefits the arrangement offered, it was obvious that he was not exactly thrilled to be lumbered with a health hazard living under his feet. Or falling on top of him.

Maybe—please—he was on a flying visit. Here today, gone tomorrow.

Maybe—more likely—he wasn't, and since the deal had been done on a handshake she didn't have a contract, or a lease, or anything other than Adele's word to save her from being thrown onto the street at a moment's notice.

Belatedly, she held her tongue. And because it was easier—and probably wiser—than attempting to stare him down, she looked around for his glasses, spotting them beneath a library table stacked with academic journals.

They were the kind of ultra-modern spectacles that had no frame, just a few rivets through the lenses to hold them together, and as she scooped them up they fell to bits in her hand.

CHAPTER TWO

BENEDICT FAULKNER said nothing, but instead opened a drawer, extracted an identical pair and tossed them onto his desk.

Were broad shoulders and blue eyes enough? Ellie wondered. Could a man be a true hero if he didn't possess a sense of humour?

It didn't look good but, prepared to be fair—Emily B was not, after all, everyone's cup of tea—she dropped the remains of his spectacles into her apron pocket and, bending over backwards to give him the benefit of the doubt, said, 'I realize that Emily Brontë is not everyone's cup of tea.'

'Heathcliff,' he assured her, confirming this, 'is psychotic, and Catherine Earnshaw is dimmer than a low energy lightbulb.'

A little harsh, she thought. But, rather than argue with him, she said, 'But the passion? What about the *passion*?'

'He's psychotically passionate and she's passionately dim?' he offered.

Realising that this was a conversation going nowhere, she didn't bother to answer but turned her attention to the book itself, and in a belated attempt to prove herself a trustworthy and useful addition to his household said, 'This is a fine early edition, Dr Faulkner. It could be quite valuable.'

He glanced up at the shelf she was supposed to have been dusting, then shrugged.

'It probably belonged to my great-grandmother.' He offered no hint as to whether he thought that would make it a treasured possession, or thought as little of his great-grandmother's taste as he did of hers. 'The one who ran away with a penniless poet.'

It was odd. While he kept saying things that were certainly meant to crush her, Ellie found herself not only *not* crushed, but positively stimulated.

'Like Elizabeth Barrett?' she enquired. After all, if his great-grandmother had run away from a comfortable home, she'd probably had very good reason. A husband who didn't have sense of humour, perhaps?

'Was Robert Browning penniless?'

'Would it have mattered?'

'What do you think?'

Oh. Right. He was a cynic.

'I think that, judging by the depth of dust up there, your great-grandmother was probably the last person to take a duster to the top shelf.'

To prove her point, she opened the book and then banged it shut, producing a small cloud of the stuff. The choking fit was not intentional, but it did go a long way to proving her point.

Dr Faulkner made no move to ease her plight—none of that back-slapping, or rushing for a glass of water nonsense for him. On the contrary, he kept a safe distance, waiting until she'd recovered, before he picked up the duster she'd dropped as she'd vainly sought to save herself and offered it to her.

Ellie used it to give the leather binding a careful wipe.

'Books,' she assured him, having clearly demonstrated the necessity, 'should be dusted at least once a year.'

'Oh? Is that what you were doing?'

Did his face warm just a little? Not with anything as definite as a smile, but surely there was the slightest shifting of the facial muscles?

'Dusting?' he added.

No, not warmth. Just sarcasm. He was a sarcastic cynic. Without a sense of humour.

Fortunately, before she could say something guaranteed to leave her with a huge empty space where the roof over her head was meant to be, the clock on the mantelpiece began to chime the half-hour, and, genuinely surprised, she exclaimed, 'Good grief! Is that right?' She looked at her own wristwatch and saw that it was it fact ten minutes slow. 'I lose all sense of time when I'm dusting a good book.'

'Perhaps you should save your energies for something less distracting?'

'No, it's okay. I'm prepared to suffer,' she assured him, wheeling the steps back into place. She didn't actually feel much like climbing them, but she'd have to do it sooner or later, and it was a bit like falling off a horse—best to get straight back on. Or so she'd heard. 'I hate to leave a job half done.'

'Very commendable, but I'd be grateful if you'd save it for another day. I have calls to make.'

Ellie ignored him. She wasn't about to scuttle off like one of his students put in her place. She'd been there, done that—although not, admittedly, with any lecturer who looked like Benedict Faulkner—and got the degree to prove it. Instead she concentrated on finishing what she'd started.

'Are you going to be much longer, Miss March?' he asked, as she worked her way along the shelf.

And that was a way of keeping his distance, too. Whoever called anyone under the age of fifty 'Miss' any more? Although, given the choice, she preferred it to 'madam'.

'My name is Gabriella,' she reminded him. Her way of keeping her distance. All her friends, employers, called her Ellie. Gabriella was a special occasion name. Gabriella March was going to look very special embossed in gold on the cover of her first book. Then, having descended the ladder—this time in the conventional manner, one step at a time—she added, 'And it's Mrs. Mrs Gabriella March.'

He removed his spectacles and turned to face her. Now she had his attention. 'Mrs? There are two of you?'

She stiffened. 'No. Just me. If you find all that too difficult to remember, maybe you'd find Ellie easier.'

She could do sarcasm.

'Ellie?'

'There—that wasn't so difficult, was it?'

Unsurprisingly, he did not respond with an invitation to call him Ben, and she found herself wishing she'd left it at 'Ellie'.

'I'll, um, leave you in peace, then. If there's nothing else I can do for you?'

His look suggested that she had done more than enough, but he restricted his response to, 'Nothing. Thank you…Ellie.'

She could tell that he'd had to force himself to use her name. Just what was his problem? It wasn't as if she'd flirted outrageously with him. Good looking he might be, give or take a sense of humour, but she wasn't about to throw herself at him. Not intentionally, anyway. Not if she wanted to continue to 'live-in'—and it was quite possible that this was just a flying visit.

'Help yourself to whatever you like from the fridge,' she said. 'Milk. Eggs…' Then, when that didn't elicit a grateful response—or any response at all… 'Right. Well, I'll see you later, perhaps.'

Dr Benedict Faulkner easily managed to contain his excitement at the possibility.

Ellie forced herself to ignore the shabby rucksack that had been dumped in the kitchen. It was probably full of dirty washing, and her fingers twitched to get it into the washing machine, but she restrained herself.

Instead she wiped a smudge from the wooden drainer, rearranged a jug full of garden flowers she'd put on the windowsill, straightened a row of old boots in the mud room. She always found it hard to drag herself away from this house. It felt lonely, as if it needed her.

Which was plainly ridiculous.

What it needed, she thought, was a couple who would love it and cherish it and fill it with children. A proper family to bring life to silent rooms, children to play *Chopsticks* on the piano, build dens in the over-grown garden. A woman with time and love to lavish on it and turn it into a home. Someone like Lady Gabriella and the imaginary family with which she'd populated it during the last few months. Eight-year-old Oliver, six-year-old Sasha, little Chloe. And a shadowy masculine figure who was not the man she'd loved, married, lost—this was not his place—but someone utterly different, a man who, until now, she'd managed to avoid bringing into focus…

Enough. Time to go. She picked up her backpack, then paused to guiltily dead-head the bedraggled pansies in a dreary stone trough by the kitchen door—something else that looked as if the last person who'd taken any notice of it was Dr Faulkner's great-grandmother.

Ben Faulkner stood at the arched gothic window of his study and watched as Ellie March struggled to mount a vintage sit-up-and-beg bike of the kind that his great-grandmother had probably ridden. The flighty one who'd read romantic fiction and caused a scandal.

If she'd been around today, he thought, she'd probably be wearing hip-hugging jeans, a cropped T-shirt and have a gold ring in her navel, too. Ellie March was not only a danger to any man who made the mistake of getting too close to the ladder she was perched on, but dressed like that she was a serious traffic hazard.

He closed his eyes, reliving the moment when he'd opened the study door and seen her whiling away the working day with her head in a book. It was as if time had somehow slipped back.

He shook his head at the stupidity of it.

Natasha had possessed an ethereal pale gold Nordic beauty that the more substantial, earthier Ellie March could never aspire to.

And Tasha would not have been wasting her time reading a nineteenth-century gothic romance, but Yevtushenko, or Turgenev. In Russian.

Yet, even while he'd known it was just an illusion, he'd still been drawn in. Like a moth to a flame.

Why couldn't his sister just mind her own business?

What arrangement had she tied him into? Whatever it was, he'd have to give the woman reasonable notice, time to find somewhere else.

It could take weeks, he thought, flexing his shoulder, easing the muscle he'd pulled as she'd felled him, then lain there, as warm and soft a handful of womanhood as any man could wish for, her hand against his heart, her hair brushing against his cheek, her scent tugging at buried memories.

He'd kept his eyes closed then, in a vain attempt to keep them from surfacing. He kept them closed now, hoping to claw them back, hold the moment.

Stupid, stupid...

And yet there was a warmth in Ellie's soft brown eyes that sparked and flared and stirred at something he'd thought long dead inside him. Something that he did not want resurrected.

Forcing himself to confront the reality, rather than some fantasy brought on by jet lag, he watched as she tried to scoot the bike into motion. She seemed to be having trouble, and as soon as she put all her weight on her leg she pulled up short, letting the bike fall. Then she aimed a heartfelt kick at it.

The kick was a mistake.

He was right, he decided, heading for the door. He should have turned around and walked away while he'd had the chance.

'Why didn't you tell me that you'd hurt your knee when you fell?'

Ellie had seen Dr Faulkner striding towards her on those long, fine legs, and her pain had been overridden by a flutter of pleasure that, had she had time to analyse it, would have brought a blush to her cheek. As soon as he opened his mouth, however, it was clear that he was no knight in armour riding to her rescue.

She lifted her shoulders a millimetre or two.

Okay, so she was no Guinevere, but even so a little sympathy would have been welcome, instead of the un-diluted irritation that appeared to be his standard response to her.

What was his problem?

She hadn't gone out of her way to get under his feet. On the contrary, he was the one who'd got under hers. He was the one who was in the wrong place at the wrong time, not her.

'My mother taught me that discretion was the better part of valour,' she said. 'It seemed like an excellent moment to put her advice to good use.'

'It might have been more useful if she'd warned you about the dangers of daydreaming at the top of ladders,' he replied.

Ellie watched as he picked up the bike and propped it against the wall, out of harm's way.

Hello! I'm here! Crumpled up on the driveway in agony—well, maybe agony was pushing it a bit, but still, it's me you're supposed to be picking up and—

Maybe not.

Having dealt with the bike, he turned to her.

'Can you stand?' he asked.

'I'm going to have to, unless I plan on staying here all evening.'

She could do 'you're a dumb idiot' responses, too.

Then, as she finally made a move, he said, 'Wait!'

She looked up at him.

'For what? Christmas?'

By way of reply, he offered her his hands.

Better. Especially as they were the kind of hands a romantic novelist expected of her hero. Broad palms. Long fingers. Wide thumb-tips. Not smooth, soft, like most academics, but callused, scarred with small cuts and abrasions. Dull red marks that looked as if they might have been burns.

It seemed almost wanton to place her own against them, but it was a gesture, one it would be rude to ignore, and she grasped them. He pulled her to her feet without making it look as if he was hauling a sack of coal from a cellar, making her feel for just a moment like some fragile heroine.

It was only the words that came out of his mouth that persistently spoiled the image.

'How is it?' he asked, finally getting even that bit right. 'Your leg?'

'Fine,' she said, feeling no pain. Then, realising that she was staring up at him instead of testing her knee, she quickly said, 'Thank you.' And let go.

For a moment she thought it was going to be all right, but then she made the mistake of twisting around to get at her backpack, and gasped as pain shot through the joint.

'That fine?' he said, catching her elbow, taking her weight as the knee buckled.

'Tricky things, knees,' she said, catching her breath. It was the knee, not the man. She did not fancy him. She was not that shallow. She had standards, and they included kindness above sun-kissed hair and cheek-bones that could slice cheese. 'Great in a straight line, not so good for cornering. But it'll be okay.'

'Of course it will.'

Now, *that*, she decided, really was sarcasm.

'Where were you going?' he asked.

'What? Oh, to the Assembly Rooms in the city centre. There's a reception for the Chamber of Commerce.'

'You're a member of the Chamber of Commerce?'

She stared at him. Was he kidding? It was impossible to tell from his expression. 'No,' she replied, taking no chances. 'I'm attending the reception in a professional capacity.' Then, in the face of his blank expression, 'I'm on waitress duty,' she explained. 'Drinks, canapés…'

'Right.' Those blue eyes swept over her in a thoughtful look. 'The dress code, if you don't mind me saying so, seems a little casual. What happened to the little black dress and white apron?'

'For your information, Dr Faulkner, they're in my backpack.' Well, the modern equivalent, anyway. Black trousers and black shirt. 'Along with the black stockings and suspenders,' she added, tossing caution to the winds. There was only so much sarcasm a girl could take with a smile. 'The police have forbidden me from wearing them when I'm riding a bike,' she added, just to demonstrate that sarcasm was not a male preserve. 'Speaking of which…' she shrugged off her backpack and extracted her cellphone '…I'd better call a cab.'

'What?' It was the second time she'd managed to grab his full attention. She was beginning to enjoy it. 'You can't seriously be planning to spend the evening on your feet? Surely they can find a replacement?'

'I *am* the replacement,' she informed him, as she scrolled through her fast-dial numbers. Waitressing at receptions was absolutely her least favourite job—including cleaning ovens. 'And I can't let Sue down.'

'Why not?' he demanded. 'Who is Sue?'

'My best friend since playgroup, despite the fact that

we're total opposites…' She found the number she was looking for and hit 'dial'. 'Which is why she's the one running Busy Bees, while I'm the one she's paying to smile and waft around gracefully with trays of drinks and canapés.'

'Not tonight.'

'Well, maybe wafting gracefully will be a stretch,' she admitted. Then, 'Damn, it's engaged.'

As she hit 'redial', he said, 'Leave it!' And, in case she had any plans to ignore him, he wrapped those long and very strong fingers around both hand and phone, so that she could do nothing but blink.

How dared he?

She looked at his hand. Then at him.

'What the hell do you think you're doing?' she demanded.

'Stopping you from behaving like an idiot.'

That would cover it, she thought. However, since it was the only option open to her, she said, 'I appreciate your concern, and if I had any choice I can assure you I wouldn't be doing this.' Then, when he didn't seem convinced, 'Truly. I had something much more interesting planned for tonight.'

For just a moment she thought he was going to ask her what, but he apparently thought better of it and instead said, 'Very well, if you insist on going then I have no choice but to drive you there myself.'

'You don't have to do that.'

'Oh, yes, Mrs March, I do.'

'Ellie, please.' Maybe she'd misjudged him…

'But not before you've got some strapping on your knee.'

'There's no time for that. I'll sort it out when I get

there,' she assured him, lying through her teeth. 'A lift is more than enough—'

'I'll do it now,' he said. 'Or I'll take you to the local hospital and let them do it.' He didn't wait for her to choose, which suggested he was a fast learner, but put his arm around her waist. It must have been shock that stilled the 'get lost; I'll take a cab' retort that flew to her lips, and made redundant his follow-up, 'How will you beat off burglars and mow the lawn if you're laid up with a crook knee?'

Pressed against the soft weave of his jacket, his arm supporting her, she felt the words still in her throat. This, she decided, must be what being swept off your feet must feel like.

'This,' she said, 'is ridiculous.'

'I agree. You should be lying down with a cold compress on your leg. Maybe if I tempted you with something from my extensive library of gothic novels you might think again?'

He could tempt her, full-stop, she thought, shocking herself, as she looked up at him. Despite the sense of humour shortfall and the high-level bossiness. She must be a lot shallower than she thought. For once, however, she managed to keep her thoughts to herself; maybe discretion, once admitted, seeped into the mind and took over.

'Any other time.' She sounded breathless. Totally pathetic…

'It's a one-time offer,' he said. Then, reluctantly, 'Oh, well, it's your knee—'

'Right.' She swallowed, gathered herself. 'So leave me to worry about it. Let's go.'

'The accident, however, was partially my fault—'

'Partially?'

He shrugged. She felt the movement, rather than saw it. 'All right, I'll take full responsibility. But I don't suppose kicking your bike improved matters.'

Oh…rhubarb-and-custard! But of course he'd seen her childish outburst, or he wouldn't be standing here now, with his arm around her waist.

'And as your employer, however unwittingly…' make that 'unwillingly' she thought '…at the moment of impact, I'm going to have to insist on some rudimentary precautions. Just in case you're unable to work for weeks and decide to sue me.'

'Now who's being ridiculous?' There went the discretion, she thought, as he gave her a look that suggested it wasn't him. 'Really! I *like* living here.' More importantly, 'Lady Gabriella' lived here; in fact she was doing a brilliant job of fixing the place up, if only on paper. Even she wasn't mad enough to re-gild frames, actually plant the herb garden she'd planned, or paint the sagging summerhouse—another coat of paint would probably bring it tumbling down. 'I love living in that ridiculous little turret.'

'You do?'

He could have tried harder to disguise his regret.

'I do.' The house inspired her. 'Why would I do anything to put that at risk?' Then, in a moment of inspiration, 'Besides, Adele is my employer, not you.'

'Since I own the house, that's debatable.'

'I know nothing about that. My agreement is with her, so I couldn't sue you, could I?' His eyes narrowed, and it occurred to her that she might have accidentally hit on the perfect delaying tactic. 'Maybe you should talk to her about it?' she suggested.

'I will.'

You can try, she thought. One of the reasons his sister

had wanted someone responsible in the house was because she didn't want to be bothered with long distance emergencies such as frozen pipes, or squatters, or tiles blowing off in a gale.

Didn't want to be bothered full-stop. In fact she'd made it perfectly clear that she thought her brother should sell the place and buy something modern and easily run, like her.

Maybe it wasn't so surprising that she'd imagined Dr Faulkner as some half-witted old bloke, lost in his books.

'Look,' she said, checking her watch, because it was so hard to think when she was looking at him, 'if we don't make a move right now, I'm going to be late.'

'Then the sooner you stop arguing,' he said, 'the better.'

With his arm about her waist she was very up-close-and-personal indeed, and his eyes warned her that she was testing his patience.

'Who's arguing?' she asked. Not that he'd bothered to wait for her to humour him. Instead, with one arm he lifted her clear off the ground so that, dangling at his side, her only option was to fling her own arms around his neck and hang on as he carried her through the front door, down the hall and into the kitchen.

Maybe 'swept off her feet' was an exaggeration, but if he had done that it would have been hideously embarrassing. Far too reminiscent of being carried over the threshold.

Besides, it was a terrific neck.

Strong, with smooth skin and a soft mane of silky hair that brushed against her bare arm. He smelt good, too. Nothing fancy, just a tweedy, leathery, totally male smell. There was no doubt about it, the man was solid hero material. He just needed to lighten up, smile once in a while.

He lowered her onto a hard kitchen chair, held her there for a moment, presumably concerned that she might spring to her feet and make a bid for freedom.

He didn't just have amazingly blue eyes, she realised, but seriously wonderful eyelashes, too.

'First-aid kit?' he prompted.

'Umm?' Then blushed furiously as she realised that it wasn't him hanging on to her. On the contrary, she was the one with her arms still around his neck, clinging on like a limpet. 'Oh. It's under the sink,' she said, using one of her arms to wave in that direction. 'A red box with a white cross…'

She managed to keep her mouth tightly closed as he sorted through the contents, found a crêpe bandage. Watched curiously, but still in silence, as he fetched a bottle of water from the fridge, filled a bowl with it. Then he dropped in the bandage.

Oh, no…

'You're not coming near me with that!'

'No?' He poked at the bandage to make sure it was thoroughly soaked in the icy water, then glanced at her. 'I thought you liked living here.'

She shouldn't have told him that, she realised belatedly. Knowledge was power. If he knew how important it really was he could use it to make her do anything.

Okay, not *anything*…

Although, actually, if he smiled…

'Can you get out of those jeans without help?' he asked.
What?

'Or would you prefer me to cut up the leg?' He held up a small pair of scissors and snipped graphically at the air with them.

'Your choice,' he prompted.

'No!' It wasn't just the fact that they were her favourite jeans that made her capitulate. Annoying as it was to have to admit it, she knew he was right. She'd never last five minutes in the scrum of a Chamber of Commerce reception without some kind of strapping on her knee. She wouldn't be doing it at all if Sue hadn't been desperate. It was her Writers' Circle night, and she was going to miss the first half of the meeting.

'Give me a minute,' she said, snapping open the button at the waist, pausing for him to turn around, give her a little privacy in which to wriggle them over her bottom.

He just waited for her to get on with it, and maybe she was being unnecessarily coy. Once they were off, they were off… Her legs would be bare and, since she was wearing a crop top, her knickers were going to be on show.

She wasn't sure whether she was relieved that she'd opted for comfortable, sensible white knickers, or sorry that she wasn't wearing her barely there special occasion scarlet thong that might just have brought a blush to his cheeks and made him regret being quite so bossy.

She let her jeans crumple in a heap around her feet, but she didn't dare kick them away and risk doing any more damage.

Apparently unmoved by the sight of her naked limbs, he eased them over her feet, tossed them over a nearby chair, and then lifted her injured leg, propping her foot against his leg while he prodded her knee, all the time watching her face to see if she flinched. But, given sufficient time to compose herself, she could keep a straight face, too. She needed it when, apparently satisfied that there was no serious damage, he used the icy bandage to bind her knee with deft efficiency.

It seemed that the shoulders weren't just for show;

he strapped up her leg with the skill of a man who knew all the moves.

'How does it feel?' he asked.

'I don't know. It's numb with cold.'

'An hour from now you'll be wishing it was still that way. Can you walk on it?'

She gripped his hand, hauled herself up, took a stiff-legged step. 'It would seem so. Good job, Doc.'

The look he gave her suggested that he did not appreciate the 'Doc', but he let it go. 'It'll help, although you'll probably find "wafting" rather difficult.' He picked up her jeans, offered them to her. 'I'll bring the car to the door while you struggle back into these.'

Ellie abandoned the jeans; since she wasn't cycling, she might as well save time by changing now. She stripped off the little crop top to reveal her favourite white lace push-'em-up bra. Such a pity it was her knee she'd strained; she'd have liked to see how straight a face Dr Faulkner could have kept with her 'wench' boobs in his face as he'd strapped her shoulder...

Grinning idiotically at the thought, she hauled her black waitressing trousers and shirt from her backpack. It was only when she was all buttoned up and ready to go that she turned—very carefully—and saw Benedict Faulkner standing in the doorway. She'd assumed he'd wait in the car for her.

Just how long had he been standing there?

'You were lying about the stockings and suspenders, then?' he said, his face straighter than a ruler.

'I charge extra for them,' she said, walking stiff-leggedly to the door, 'and the Chamber of Commerce is cheap...' She stifled a gasp. 'I was expecting Adele's Morris Minor,' she said. It had been tucked up during her absence, in her brother's garage. Unlike this stunningly beautiful vintage sports car. 'Where did this come from?'

'I left it with a colleague while I was away.'

'Someone you trust, obviously?' she said as, unable to bend one leg, she was reduced to flopping backwards into the low seat, then lifting her stiff leg into the car.

'Obviously.'

'The fact that you took the time to reclaim it suggests you're going to be around for a while.'

'I stayed with her for a couple of days while I caught up on sleep,' he said. 'But you're right. I won't be going anywhere in the next week or two.'

Her.

She had oddly mixed feelings about that. She concentrated on the 'oh bother' variety, and spent the regrettably short ride into the city dwelling miserably on the horrors of flat-hunting.

'What time shall I pick you up?' he asked, as he pulled up in front of the Assembly Rooms.

'What? Oh, there's no need for that,' she said, opening the door, then belatedly realising that, while flopping backwards had worked to get into the car, she was going to need rather more help getting out. 'I'm going on to a meeting next door,' she said, as he climbed out, walked around the car. 'At the library. I'm sure someone will give me a lift home.'

Having offered her a hand, he made no immediate move to help her out. Instead he said, 'How sure?'

Actually, very sure, but with his hand wrapped around hers she seemed to have trouble in breathing.

Taking her hesitation as not-very-sure-at-all, he

repeated the question. 'What time shall I pick you up from the library?'

'We, um, usually go down the pub afterwards,' she managed.

'Your life is one social whirl, Ellie.'

'What can I say?'

'If you're ever going to get out of this car, I'd suggest you tell me what time I should pick you up at the library.'

She was torn between fury at his dictatorial manner and a certain undeniable pleasure at the idea of being collected from the meeting by a dishy man in a seriously good-looking car.

Besides, he was right. She was entirely at his mercy. If he didn't help her out of the car she'd be stuck there with him all evening. Or, more accurately, he'd be stuck with her.

Oh, the temptation…

Dismissing the idea as unworthy—and because she was already late—she said, 'Okay, Doc, you win.'

'Ben,' he said. 'Just…Ben.'

'Ben. Nine, then. At the library.'

Satisfied, he eased her from the car and saw her safely up the steps and inside the Assembly Rooms. It was only then that she allowed herself a self-satisfied little grin. First objective achieved. He'd asked her to call him Ben.

Her next target was a smile. Entirely for his own good, naturally…

CHAPTER THREE

ELLIE'S pleasure was short-lived. The reception was noisy, crowded, and went on well beyond eight. By the time she'd helped clear up and got to the library it was nearly nine, and most of the members had already decamped to the pub.

Diana Sutton, the group's secretary, who was already locking up, was sympathetic. 'Bad luck. Never mind, come and have a drink. We're celebrating. Gary's sold a short story and Lucy's sold an article to *Women's World*. The one she wrote when we did that magazine exercise.'

'Really? That's brilliant news!'

'Did you ever do anything for *Milady*?'

Ellie, who'd had to force her excitement through an unexpectedly large lump in her throat, found herself floundering. She'd written her journal to prove to everyone that she could do anything she set her mind to, but, having succeeded with it beyond her wildest dreams, it was the one thing she couldn't brag about.

What, she wondered, was the point of belonging to a support group, with people who sympathised with your rejections, cheered at your successes, if you weren't totally engaged? Honest.

These were her friends…

'No? Well, it was a bit of a joke,' Diana said, taking her silence as a no and rescuing her from having to admit that she was a failure.

Sean's friends.

He was the one who'd written poetry. This had been his scene. She'd gone along because that was what they did. Sean-and-Ellie. Ellie-and-Sean. Started writing her historical romance because—well, she'd had to do something. No one, least of all Sean, had ever taken it seriously…

'I'm sorry,' Diana said, to someone who'd followed her in. 'The library is closed. Late night is tomorrow.'

'Thanks, but I've just come to pick up Ellie.'

Ellie half turned, happier to see Ben Faulkner than she would have believed possible a couple of hours ago. There was no way she could sit in the pub with these people tonight and not feel a complete fraud.

'Good timing, Doc,' she said. Then, 'I'll have to give the pub a miss tonight, Diana. Tell Lucy and Gary that I'm green with envy, will you?'

'I will,' she said, her look speculative, as if trying to work out how someone with so little to offer in the way of looks, style and career prospects had managed to pull someone so fanciable. Clocking all the details so that she could tell the rest of the group. 'See you next month, then?'

'Work permitting,' she said, knowing that she wouldn't go. Couldn't go. She hadn't actually lied, but by not telling the truth she'd cut herself off from them. Cut herself off from her past.

Too miserable to think, she allowed Ben to help her down the steps, across the pavement. He must have remembered the inelegant way she'd flopped into the seat, and this time he supported her, lowering her in gently— no doubt thinking of his springs or suspension or whatever it was that men worried about when it came to their precious cars.

She tugged on the seat belt, glancing back as it refused to budge.

'Gently,' Ben said, sliding behind the wheel and then, when 'gently' wouldn't do it, 'Leave it to me!' And he reached across to pull it smoothly over her body, giving Ellie a dizzying close-up of his profile, a whiff of undiluted masculinity, before he fitted it into the clip.

'It's a bit temperamental,' he said, catching her look, misunderstanding it.

'It's old; it's entitled to be cranky,' she said.

'True. So what's your excuse?'

'None of your damn business.' She was tired, irritable, and at that moment she didn't like herself very much. Which apparently made two of them. 'I did tell you I'd get a lift.'

'Next time,' he replied coldly, 'I'll listen.'

'Believe me,' she snapped back, 'I don't plan to do this again any time soon.' And it wasn't the knee she was referring to.

'No?' He did not appear to be convinced.

'No.' Then, 'Oh, look, I'm sorry. I've had the kind of evening I'll be glad to forget, but that's no reason to take it out on you.' He didn't answer. 'Or your car,' she added.

He turned to her, his face creased not with irritation but concern. 'Is the leg painful? We could go straight to A&E if you think it needs professional treatment?'

'No. It held up better than I deserved for mistreating it so badly. I hardly felt a twinge. You did a good job,

Doc. Ben,' she corrected hurriedly, and, because she'd been at best tetchy, at worst downright rude, 'I'm grateful for the lift, truly. I'll be glad to get home.' Realising that was probably not what he wanted to hear, 'How about you? Any long-term damage?'

'I'll live.' He glanced across at her. 'Why do you do this, Ellie? Waitress, clean, caretake? You're obviously an intelligent woman—'

'Despite my deplorable taste in fiction?'

'We all have our weaknesses.'

Ellie didn't consider her love of nineteenth-century literature a weakness, but since there was no likelihood of changing Ben Faulkner's mind she said, 'True. So what's yours?'

He glanced at her. 'Do you always say the first thing that comes into your head?'

'Usually,' she admitted.

'And you've managed to live how long? Twenty-four, twenty-five years without coming to serious harm?'

'It's very rude to ask a woman her age.' Then, 'Twenty-six years, actually.'

'Twenty-six? Amazing.'

'I know. I'm very well preserved.' No wonder Mrs Cochrane thought she'd been married before the ink on her A-level certificates was dry. 'All that beeswax in the furniture polish, no doubt.'

'I meant it's amazing that you've survived unscathed.'

She lifted one shoulder a fraction. 'No one reaches my age unscathed,' she said. The wounds might not show, but they went deep.

Fortunately, he thought she was talking about her knee, and said, 'Can't you find a less painful way of keeping body and soul together?'

'If you think teaching a class of thirteen-year-olds to appreciate the Classics is not painful, you should try it some time.'

'You're a teacher?'

'Not any more. Now I'm a writer.' Then, because he didn't seem unduly impressed—and why should he be?—she added, 'That was the local Writers' Circle meeting I missed tonight.'

'And you missed it for the pleasure of carrying heavy trays of drinks because you couldn't let your friend down?' He glanced across at her. 'What does she do for you?'

'She employs me. Even writers have to eat.'

'Actually, until you're earning a living from writing, I'd suggest that you're a waitress.'

'That's like saying Vincent van Gogh wasn't a painter because he didn't make a living from his work. Not that I'm comparing myself with him,' she added quickly. Then, because it was clear he was not convinced, 'Besides, I'm not unpublished. Far from it. I've had articles published. Short stories. I'll have you know…'

Just in time she caught her runaway mouth.

'What?'

'Nothing.' He glanced across at her. She shrugged. 'If you must know, I've written a novel.'

Well, she had to say something.

'Would I have read it?'

'It's being considered by an agent…' that would be agent number eleven '…at this very moment.'

'Then the answer is no. I imagine it's a romance?' he said. And she could have sworn she saw him finally crack a smile.

'What's wrong with romance?' she demanded. That

was definitely not the smile she was looking for. 'Jane Austen wrote romance.'

'So she did. And your beloved Emily Brontë. Brooding, arrogant men, brought to their knees by strong-minded young women.'

'Sounds good to me.'

'But unlikely.'

'Not that unlikely.' Ben Faulkner had a pretty good line in disdain himself. 'I felled you without even trying.'

'I had always assumed, in romantic terms, the felling to be metaphorical,' he said.

'It is. Pity. The other way is so much quicker.' Then, hurriedly, 'Not that it was intentional.' She was quite happy to see him on his feet if he'd only let her stay on in his house. There was tons of room, after all, and she earned her keep. Besides, he was bound to be going away again soon...

'Can't you write and teach?' he asked, clearly no more anxious than her to prolong that line of thought.

'You've been talking to my father, haven't you?'

'Is that what he thinks?'

'Pretty much. Of course he helped finance me through four years of university, and has every right to expect me to put my education to the purpose for which it was intended. Teaching, as he never tires of telling me, is the perfect job for a woman.'

'A career that fits around family ties? That's a touch patronising.'

'He'd say he was being realistic. The hours, nine to three-thirty, and the long holidays would, according to him, give me plenty of time to write in my spare time.'

And he thought *she* lived in a fantasy world.

'Fathers, patronising or not, tend to have the best

interests of their offspring at heart.' He glanced at her. 'He can't be very happy with what you're doing.'

'No.' More guilt that his aspirations for her had been so cruelly dashed. But she couldn't help it. 'The thing is, Ben, that while cleaning, waitressing, helping out people who need a spare pair of hands occasionally, may not be an intellectually rewarding career, not something that Dad wants to boast about to his buddies at the golf club, it does have its good points.'

'It does?'

'Absolutely. For instance, apart from the occasional bag of ironing, I never have to take work home with me. I don't have to spend my weekends marking. There are no lesson plans to prepare, and the paperwork is practically zero.'

She started early, and even while she polished, ironed and vacuumed her mind was her own, free to take imaginary journeys, live a different life in her head.

'I start at seven, I'm usually finished by two. Then I have a clear run through until bedtime to write,' she explained.

'Even so…'

'Life is too short, too uncertain to put dreams on hold, Ben.' She glanced at him. 'Losing Sean, my husband, taught me that. I don't want to look back and say "I wish…". I'm taking the balloon ride.'

She felt rather than saw his look as he absorbed the information that she was a widow rather than just another girl who'd married in haste and lived to repent it, as so many of her friends had done.

'The balloon ride?' he repeated, after a moment.

She couldn't believe she'd said that out loud. Maybe it was the fall, or the painful realisation of just how cut off she'd become from her family, her friends, that had brought the words bubbling to the surface now.

'We used to watch them, the hot air balloons, drifting along the valley on summer evenings. Sean wanted to book a champagne ride for our first anniversary, but the electricity bill had arrived and I said...'

She shook her head, not wanting to think about what she'd said.

'I'd spent my entire life doing the sensible thing, choosing the solid degree in English over some airy-fairy notion of taking Art. Waiting to get married until I finished university, had my teaching qualification.' Putting babies on hold until they could afford them...

'What happened to him?' She looked up. 'Sean?'

'Oh, it was one of those ordinary Sundays. We got up, had a row about the fact that he'd used all the milk in a midnight raid on the fridge. He told me not to get excited, put on his headphones, jogged off to the newsagent's to fetch a pint...'

They had come to a halt at traffic lights and she knew that Ben was looking at her.

'He bought a paper, was looking at the sports head-lines instead of the road. He always did that. Jogged there, walked back reading the paper, quite incapable of waiting until he got home to find out how Melchester United were doing in the league. He was football mad. I was always telling him he'd walk into something...'

He'd used to laugh, tease her that she was turning into a nagging wife...

'He stepped off the pavement without looking. The driver never stood a chance.' Then, 'Someone ran to fetch me...'

For a moment she was back there with Sean, kneeling

in the road, milk and blood soaking into the triumphant headlines proclaiming that United would move up next season. Cradling him in her arms as he said, 'We aren't going to get our balloon ride, Ellie...'

Then, as the car behind them hooted impatiently, she snapped back to the present, turned to him, and said, 'You can't stop time and re-do the bits you got wrong. The bits you missed.'

'I'm sorry.'

Sorry he'd asked...

'It was three years ago,' she said, used to people lost for words, unable to cope with her loss. As if time made it any easier. Then, briskly, 'What about you, Ben? What's your life plan?'

He raised his hand in apology to the driver behind, pulled away, said, 'Can you plan life? When so much is out of your control?'

'Maybe not, but you shouldn't be passive. Wait for things to happen to you. Keep putting stuff off until the time is right.'

'Carpe diem?'

'Exactly! Seize the day. That's what I told my father when I gave up teaching.'

'And what did he say?'

'He said that fish were damn slippery things and I'd be better occupied sorting out a pension plan.'

Ben Faulkner laughed. She turned and stared at him. Mistaking her startled reaction for offence, he shook his head, 'I'm sorry. I didn't mean...'

'It's okay. I laughed too.' Although suddenly it wasn't so funny. Even when things went right it wasn't always as 'right' as it might be. Witness her *Milady* column.

Finally she had something to show for all her hard work—but who could she tell? Share it with? Not her sceptical father who, proud as Punch, would buy copies of the magazine and give them to everyone he knew. Not her mother who, even sworn to secrecy, wouldn't be able to resist sharing the news with her best friend, which would be the equivalent of placing an ad in the *Courier.*

She hadn't even told Sue. Her own very best friend. The one person with whom she'd shared every secret of her heart.

Only Stacey knew, and she wouldn't tell. Although she and her sister had precious little in common, they did know how to keep each other's secrets.

'Adele wasn't expecting you back until next year,' she said, not wanting to think about the kind of person she was turning into. 'What happened to your plans?'

'Riots, mayhem, civil disturbance. I was working in Kirbeckistan.'

'But isn't that where…?' She recalled the graphic scenes of violence she'd seen on the news. 'But the civil war started weeks ago. Where have you been?' Then, 'Did you have trouble getting out?'

He shrugged. 'When it finally blew, it all happened very quickly, and the airport was overrun before anyone could get away. A group of us walked out over the mountains. It took a while.'

'That must have been tough.'

It certainly explained the state of his hands.

'Not as tough for me as for the poor devils who had to stay there,' he said. 'The political situation being what it was, I'd taken the precaution of scanning and sending back the texts I was working on via the internet, so they're not totally lost. I can at least continue my work here at the university.'

'Are they important?'

'They take us back another thousand years.'

'And you can read them?'

That did produce a smile. 'Let's say that it's a work in progress.'

'It can't be the same as having the original documents to refer to,' she sympathised.

'No.'

'But it'll be over in a few weeks, won't it?' she said hopefully. 'You'll be able to go back, carry on?'

He turned into the drive, pulled up by the kitchen door.

'I can understand your eagerness to see the back of me, Ellie, but since the rebels burned the museum down around me I fear that your optimism is misplaced.'

She'd been right about the burns, then. 'Were you hurt?'

'Nothing to make a fuss about.'

His jaw tightened momentarily, and she was sure that other people he knew hadn't been so lucky. He didn't linger to discuss it, however, but climbed out and came round to open the door and help her to her feet. For a moment he continued to hold both of her hands, steadying her.

'Are you okay?' he asked. 'Will you be able to manage the stairs?'

'I'll be fine,' she said.

She'd have to be. Besides, she wanted him to know that she wouldn't be a nuisance, wouldn't be continually under his feet.

'Thank you again for the lift. And the first aid.'

He nodded, picked up her bag and handed it to her.

'You must have washing,' she continued—Miss

Runaway Mouth of whatever year you'd care to mention. 'If you leave it in the utility room, I'll run it through the machine tomorrow.'

'I do know how to use my own washing machine.'

'Do you? How rare is that?' When he didn't respond to her pathetic attempt at humour, she said, 'Well, the offer is there. I start very early, so I'll be gone before you get up I imagine. But you'll find all the basics—cereals, eggs, that sort of thing. For breakfast. Just help yourself.'

'Food, washing. Anything else?'

'Well, I'm in town most mornings, so if there's anything you need just stick a note on the fridge door before you go to bed,' she said, ignoring the edge to his voice that hadn't been there a few moments earlier. 'I can pick it up while I'm out.'

'And shopping. Domesticity on tap,' he said. 'For a price.'

'I'll bet my time is cheaper than yours,' she said, furious that he'd wilfully chosen to misunderstand her. There was no way she would expect him to pay for what little extra work he'd cause, and she certainly didn't expect to be paid for picking up the odd steak with her own shopping. It was obvious, however, that he thought she was just trying to capitalise on his presence, or even ingratiate herself, when she was just being herself.

He couldn't possibly think…

'Sweatshop labourers in the Far East earn more an hour than the average writer,' he said. 'Even most of the published ones.'

'Fortunately, under normal circumstances, shopping and ironing come at domestic goddess rates, which are considerably above the minimum wage,' she replied, doing her best to keep her tone civil.

'And under abnormal ones?'

Apparently he could.

'You're the one with the big brain around here, Dr Faulkner. I suggest you work it out for yourself.' She detached herself from his supporting grasp. 'Goodnight.'

She didn't linger in the kitchen. She had a kettle in her study, with a bottomless supply of instant hot chocolate—it would take at least two mugs and a raid on the biscuit tin to make her feel better after that nasty little exchange.

Did he think her story about Sean had been no more than a cheap bid for sympathy? That she would stoop to offering the full range of personal services to keep a roof over her head?

Damn it, now she had no choice but to leave.

She switched on the kettle, found a packet of double chocolate chip cookies and tipped them into the tin she kept in the top drawer of her desk.

Her plan had been to use the time she'd gained from missing out on the pub making a start on next month's *Milady* column. In her last column she'd concentrated on the garden, describing—amongst other things—her 'hands-on' restoration of an ancient bench. Well, she'd made a start—enough to make her description of aching back and need for a manicure authentic. Sent a drawing of it and the stone trough, transformed from a sad pansy dump into something ancient and venerable and overflowing with fashionable ferns similar to one she'd spotted in a shady corner in a neighbour's garden.

This month 'Lady Gabriella' was organising an *al fresco* dinner party for her anniversary, and her jottings were going to include the shopping, the preparations, the menu—all of which was going to strain simple

Ellie March's imagination to its limits; but not as far as imagining a proper smile, a hint of graciousness from Ben Faulkner.

Instead she found a copy of the local newspaper and started searching through the 'Accommodation to Let' column.

Ben didn't hurry into the house. Ellie was bound to be in the kitchen, making a drink or a sandwich. Would no doubt offer to make him something.

Or maybe not.

She'd really got to him with her 'balloon trip' story, her dead husband—which had no doubt been her intention—and he'd had to reach deep for some way to stop her lively tongue. Make her drop the 'Doc', drop the 'Ben', revert to a very chilly 'Dr Faulkner'. In the end she'd made it easy for him, with her eagerness to please, but, taking no chances, he put the car away and then went for a walk in the garden.

A grey cat appeared out of the darkness, mewed softly as it brushed against his legs, then, as a light came on at the highest level of the ridiculous little turret at the far end of the house—and, no, he was not in the least bit surprised that his romantically inclined house-sitter had claimed the most inconvenient part of the house as her own—it turned away, bounded up onto the water-butt.

He watched as the creature leapt lightly onto the roof of the porch before taking what was clearly a well-trodden path across the rising levels of the roof until, with a final leap, it gained the sill of Ellie's open window.

He saw the animal pause, back-lit by the soft light, lift its head. Heard its soft chirrup. A disembodied hand stretched out to him, and its head butted into her palm before it stepped inside. For a moment Ben felt as if he, rather than Ellie March, was the interloper. As if, despite the soft warmth of the May night, he was standing out in the cold, looking up at a room filled with warmth and comfort.

That if she had been offering a warm bed as well as a warm heart in return for a roof over her head he was all kinds of a fool to have turned her down.

Ellie couldn't concentrate. She'd looked up as Millie had appeared at her window, seen the distant shadowy figure of Ben Faulkner standing alone in the twilight of the garden, and the anger had seeped out of her.

He'd obviously been through a rough time. To come home and find himself invaded must have been the last straw.

This was his house and, tough as it was going to be to leave, she could no more impose herself on him against his wishes than fly to the moon. She'd leave him a note in the morning, tell him that she'd started looking for somewhere, that she'd move out as quickly as she could.

She was well into her second cup of chocolate, digging deep into the double-choc-chip cookies, when there was a tap on the door.

Ben heard a scuffle, the sound of drawer being slammed shut, then Ellie's muffled voice saying, 'Come in.'

He opened the door, ducked his head beneath the low lintel, stopped as he caught sight of the local paper open at the 'Accommodation to Let' section, the telltale circles around three or four of the small ads. She was, evidently, way ahead of him.

'Am I disturbing you?'

'Since the moment you walked into the library,' she replied.

'We have that in common, at least.'

'Then why are you here? I have to tell you if you're looking for anything other than a sachet of hot chocolate you're going to be disappointed.'

He was here to tell her that he'd give her a month, six weeks at the most, to find somewhere else to live. That she appeared to be ahead of him had rather taken the wind out of his sails, and instead he looked around.

The room had once been his. A teenage bolthole, study, a private place of his own, where his father, his grown-up sister hadn't been allowed. All a very long time ago.

The last time he'd been up here the room had looked tired, shabby. Abandoned.

All that had changed. Ellie had taken down the ancient curtains and left the deep window embrasure unadorned, so that the twilight sky was a deep blue arch. There were scented flowers in a cream jug with a red heart. A pinboard with a year-planner, postcards, notes, photographs of interiors, clothes, faces that had been cut from magazines. She'd brought up a colourful rug that had once been in the nursery, polished up the small desk. Thrown an embroidered shawl over the shabby sofa.

The effect was of a somewhat disordered but nevertheless inviting charm.

'You've made this comfortable,' he said, resisting the call of the sofa. He remembered exactly how it felt to stretch out on it wrapped around a girl…

'I'll put back the curtains before I go,' she said quickly, seeing him glance at the window. 'I took them down to wash them, and then decided I liked it better without.'

'I'm surprised they didn't fall to pieces.'

'No! That's not why… I was very careful.'

'I don't doubt it, but you're right. The window looks better that way. In fact the whole house looks better than it has in a long while. Very well cared for. Mrs Turner did a good job, but…'

'It's easier when you live in. There are always things that you just never get around to when you're under pressure of time.'

'Yes, I imagine so.'

'It's a lovely house.'

Ellie looked for a moment as if she was going to say something else.

'But?' he prompted. 'A bit large for one person? Is that what you were going to say?'

'I…' She shook her head. 'I was going to say that I enjoy looking after it. But, yes, it does need a family to fill it. Not that it's any of my business.'

'No, it isn't.'

'Was there something?' she asked. 'I don't imagine you climbed all the way up here simply to admire the view.'

'No…' He dragged his fingers through hair that badly needed cutting. This was not going as he'd intended. 'I just wanted you to know, to tell you, that I don't expect you to move out at a moment's notice simply because my plans have changed.'

'That's just as well, because a moment's notice would leave me sitting on the street surrounded by my stuff.'

'You haven't got anywhere? Anyone you could move in with?'

Her look spoke volumes. 'Not "at a moment's notice", but as quickly as possible—is that it?'

That had been his intention…

'What about your parents?' he asked.

'Would you move in with yours?' she demanded.

'I don't have that option.'

'I'm sorry, but neither do I. I'm well beyond the age where I'm prepared to run home to Mother.' Then, 'I imagine Sue would let me sleep on her sofa, if you insist on me leaving straight away.'

'No.' No matter how much seeing her here, so perfectly in tune with the setting—an out-of-date romantic in a ridiculous folly—stirred up buried memories, no matter how badly he wanted her out of his house, he just couldn't bring himself to say the words. 'No need for that,' he said. 'How long, realistically, do you think it will take you to find somewhere to live?'

'Realistically? Have you any idea how hard is to find decent rented accommodation in a university city packed with students?' She didn't wait for him to answer, but indicated the paper lying on the desk. 'I'll start looking tomorrow. You have my assurance that I won't drag it out.'

'Thank you,' he said, somehow wishing that, rather than being so reasonable, she'd leapt in to demand—as she had every right to—he keep to the last letter of whatever contract she'd made with Adele. That way he might not feel quite so bad. 'If you need any help with a deposit—'

'No! Thank you, Dr Faulkner. I haven't squandered the rent I've saved in the last three months.'

About to remind her that she was supposed to call him Ben, he let it go. The space was too intimate, the girl too unexpectedly appealing.

'No. Well, I'll leave you to get on, then.'

'Doc…'

He paused in the doorway, looked back.

She pushed back a strand of dark hair that had fallen over her face. 'I meant what I said about helping yourself to whatever you find in the kitchen. I promise there are no strings attached.'

CHAPTER FOUR

'BEN!' Kitty, Adele's secretary, greeted him with real warmth. 'How lovely to see you.' Then, 'Well, probably not for you. Was it very bad? Did you have any trouble getting out?'

'Yes, and yes, but I'm here and in one piece.' He hadn't encountered serious physical violence until he'd got home and Ellie March had fallen on him.

'Glad to be home, no doubt. Is everything all right?'

'The house is fine. Unfortunately, I appear to have a tenant.'

'Ellie? Oh, Lord, I hadn't thought about that. Is it going to be a problem?'

'I don't know,' he said. She'd said she'd look for somewhere else, but she'd have to pay a market rent, and in her shoes he wouldn't be in any great hurry. 'What's the deal?'

'She works for Adele, you know. Ellie is a real find, and she was so good when Adele had 'flu last January. Called in three times a day, did all her shopping and laundry. Made sure she was eating.'

'I imagine she was paid for her trouble?'

'Have you any idea how much that amount of time and care would cost?' Kitty shook her head, clearly expecting no response. 'She's paid to clean the apartment for four hours a week. When Adele was sick she did that because it was her job. The rest she did in her own time, because she's a thoroughly good person.'

'No one is that good,' he said. 'Whose idea was it for her to move into Wickham Lodge?'

'You're suggesting she had it all worked out? Was kind to Adele out of some ulterior motive?'

'She took over from Mrs Turner, knew the house was going to be empty for twelve months…'

Kitty straightened her shoulders. A bad sign.

'You can't leave a house like that empty, Ben. There's always something that needs seeing to, and when you took off without a moment's warning—well, your sister was the one who had to chase around finding people to fix things. Broken gutters. A loose slate—'

'Why on earth didn't she send me an e-mail if it was too much for her? Why didn't you? I could have organised a management agency—'

'Oh, please! She'd give me hell if she knew I was telling you this. You're more son to her than brother. You know that.'

He dragged his fingers through his hair. 'You're making me feel a complete heel, Kitty.'

'I don't mean to. I just wanted you to understand why, when Ellie's creep of a landlord started calling at all hours, making it clear that he would overlook the rent in return for a more personal arrangement—'

He managed to catch the expletive, shook his head at her look of query.

'Well, as I said, Ellie needed somewhere quickly, and Adele was at her wits' end because she was committed to this six-month field-trip in Samoa.'

'Ellie mentioned something about it.' Although she appeared to have missed Samoa from her list of possible destinations.

'Anyway, the coincidence was serendipitous, and it was all at Adele's suggestion rather than any underhand wheedling by Ellie.' She suddenly looked anxious. 'It isn't going to be problem, is it? Adele didn't expect you back until next year. To be honest, she was hoping that Ellie would use the time to get this writing bug out of her system and by then she'd be ready to go back to teaching.'

'Making life easy for her is a strange way to go about it.'

'Not really. The sooner she discovers that she's wasting her time, the sooner she'll give up.'

Perversely, his sister's lack of confidence in Ellie's talent irritated him, too. 'How do you know she's wasting her time?'

'If she isn't, Adele will have helped her on her way. A win-win situation.'

'Maybe so, but my sister doesn't have to share her house with a total stranger.'

'It's a big house, Ben.'

'I know, but Ellie somehow manages to fill every corner of it,' he said.

There was a mound of post waiting on the doormat when Ellie got home next day, so Ben Faulkner must have left for the university hard on her heels. It was just as well, since there was a large padded envelope from *Milady*, addressed to Lady Gabriella March, which would have taken some explaining.

Having done her research, she now knew that the courtesy title of 'Lady' was one given to the daughter of a peer—hence 'Lady Gabriella March' as opposed to 'Lady March'.

She just hoped Mrs Cochrane had better things to do with her time than waste it scouring *Debrett's* in a hunt for any peer with a daughter called Gabriella.

She picked up the envelope, along with the rest of the mail and took it through to the kitchen, where she'd dumped the shopping. She flipped on the kettle, and while it was boiling she sorted the envelopes into piles.

There was one large square white envelope—very stiff, obviously an invitation—addressed to Dr Benedict Faulkner. It clearly hadn't taken long for word to get around that he was back. He was a very eligible bachelor; she had no doubt that he'd be much in demand. She put that to one side to leave on his desk, then dealt with the stuff addressed to her.

Once she'd sorted through the usual junk mail begging her to borrow money, promising her dirt-cheap car insurance, offering her credit cards at nought per cent interest if only she would transfer her business to them and tossed it into the bin, all that remained, apart from the *Milady* envelope, was a reminder from her dentist that it was time for a check-up and a large brown envelope that she had addressed to herself several weeks earlier but had hoped never to see again.

No doubt about what this one contained: the first three chapters of her novel and a 'thanks-but-no-thanks' letter from yet another agent.

It wasn't that she was pessimistic by nature. No pessimist ever wrote an entire novel hoping a publisher would be sufficiently impressed to invest in its publication. Ellie had, however, sold enough small pieces of writing to have learned that when someone wanted to buy your work they didn't send it back; they phoned, or e-mailed, or sent a letter inviting you for a 'chat'.

She wasn't being pessimistic, just realistic, but she still needed to get used to the idea before she opened the envelope.

Some rejections were completely impersonal—pre-printed on a tiny slip of paper with no comment. Some came in the form of an encouraging letter—the 'this is good, but not for us' rejection.

Some agents were actually kind enough to offer to read anything else she wrote, although on bad days she suspected they had their fingers crossed that she would be too discouraged to bother.

She needed to be prepared, with a mug of tea and a full biscuit tin, before she found out which category this one fell into, so, ignoring it, she ripped open the padded envelope from *Milady*. It contained a sheaf of letters, held together with a large clip.

What on earth…? It couldn't be! Not *fan mail*.

It wasn't.

It was, instead, a bunch of letters from readers wanting details of the ferns she'd planted in the stone trough. Wanting to know how she managed to make cherry cake without the cherries sinking to the bottom—duh! Easy, when all you had to do was write about it and then draw a picture of one like her mother made. Asking where they could buy the fabric playhouse—a stripy big-top made by one of her clients that hung from the branch of a tree—that she'd sketched for her last column. Asking her advice on a suitable wedding gift for someone who'd been married before and didn't need anything for her home. Good grief, had the woman no imagination?

There was a note from Mrs Cochrane.

Well done! I've ordered some notepaper for you with the Milady *address. It should arrive in a day or two, with a supply of stamps for your replies— keep a record, please. I've cleared some space in the next issue to publish the answers to the most asked questions, and have marked the ones I plan to use.*

Can you also let me have a list of the ferns you recommend for planting in a container by Monday lunchtime at the latest. Since there was so much interest, I'm arranging a special 'reader offer' in conjunction with a specialist nursery—something you should mention in your replies.

You can send me the replies for publication with your copy for the next issue.

Forget Gabriella March, bestselling novelist. Meet 'Lady Gabriella', the lifestyle guru who was about to become homeless, she thought, as she stuffed the letters back into the envelope.

She'd just dropped a teabag into a mug when the back door opened and Ben Faulkner walked in.

'I won't be a minute,' she said, quickly covering the *Milady* envelope with her returned manuscript. 'I'm just putting away my shopping.' Then, forcing herself not to leap to do it herself, she said, 'Drop a teabag into a mug, if you like. The kettle's nearly boiled.' And carried on sorting through the vegetables and putting them in the chiller drawer of the fridge. 'Your post is on the table.'

He picked up the envelope addressed to him, his gaze lingering for a moment on the large brown envelope as he flipped it open. It might as well have had 'rejected' stamped across it in letters six inches high.

'Okay. I'm done,' she said quickly, before he could

make some sarcastic comment and provoke her into an injudicious response.

He tossed the gold-edged card—an invitation to a wedding—on the table and reached for a mug, standing shoulder to shoulder with her at the counter as he spooned coffee into a cafetière while she made her tea. Too close. Much too close.

She barely waited for the teabag to colour the water before she dumped it in the bin, scooped up her mail and, clutching it protectively to her chest, headed for the door. Then, remembering something, she put the cup down again while she searched through her bag.

'Ellie…'

'Hold on.' He was going to ask her if she'd done anything about flat-hunting—or, worse, say that he'd changed his mind, that she had to leave straight away. Before he could actually say the words, she took a small soft sleeve of bubble wrap from her bag and placed it on the table. 'Your glasses,' she said.

He looked at them, then at her. 'You had them repaired?' He sounded irritated rather than grateful.

'What did you think I was going to do with them?' she asked. Then shook her head. Obviously he thought this was another ploy to gain his sympathy, show him what a fool he'd be to let her go. 'I do the occasional stint at the optician in the High Street,' she explained. 'When his regular cleaner is away. He put them back together for me. No charge.' Then, because she was going to have to face it sooner or later, and while later was preferable, sooner was probably wiser, 'You were saying?'

He shook his head. 'Nothing. Only that you don't have to rush off on my account.'

'I've got things to do. Calls to make. Flats to look at,' she couldn't help adding.

The kitchen stilled. From somewhere in the house a clock began to chime.

Despite Kitty's intercession on Ellie's behalf, Ben had no intention of reversing his decision. It had been made, the words said. She'd accepted it without a fuss. No problem.

In theory.

The reality was that if she'd given him hell he'd have felt less like someone kicking a puppy. But if she was the kind of woman Kitty believed her to be she wouldn't do that. She'd behave like a thoroughly decent person and accept that the situation had changed. That his house no longer needed a 'sitter'.

But even a thoroughly decent person was entitled to show her feelings.

'You're very direct, Ellie,' he said.

A shadow seemed to cross her bright face and she shook her head, just once, before she lifted her chin and said, 'You didn't think that last night.'

'Last night you appeared to be offering just about everything but the kitchen sink in return for a roof over your head.'

'I did nothing of the sort!' she exclaimed, her furious blush leaving him in no doubt that she'd understood his meaning.

'No. My mistake. For which I apologise. Adele's secretary explained why you had to leave your last flat. In fact she gave you a very fine character reference.'

'You checked up on me?'

'In my shoes, wouldn't you have done the same?

You might have simply spotted an empty house and moved in for all I knew.'

'Well, at least you've been able to set your mind at rest,' she said stiffly. 'Now, if there's nothing else—?'

'Will you stand still for a moment and let me finish?' he demanded as she swept towards the door. She froze, her back to him. 'When I said you need not rush off…'

She half turned. Waited.

'When I said that, I meant…' He didn't know what he'd meant.

A pair of fine dark brows drew together in a frown.

'Just…take your time,' he said. 'Find somewhere that suits you. Where you'll feel comfortable,' he added, belatedly wishing he'd let her go.

'Is that it?'

'Yes. No. In case you were wondering, your job here is not in question.'

'Of course not. We both know how hard it is to find a good cleaner.'

'Ellie…'

'Could you sound any less enthusiastic?' she demanded. Then, 'I suppose I owe these concessions to a little arm-twisting from Kitty?'

'She didn't bother with my arms. She went straight for the withers.' This time her eyebrows went up instead of sideways. 'She gave me chapter and verse of the way you cared for Adele when she was sick,' he said.

'Adele is not just an employer, she's a friend. Leave or stay, I'd do it again tomorrow.'

'Then you must stay or go as you please,' he said, and, recalling his disparaging remarks about romantic heroines bringing arrogant men to their knees, he found himself unexpectedly in sympathy with them.

'What the devil does that mean?'

'It means...' He shook his head, unable to believe he'd got himself into this position. 'It means that I'm not going to be rid of you for at least a month, more likely two. I imagine by then I'll have got used to you.' He was doing this for Adele, he told himself. Because she'd expect nothing less of him and he owed it to her. For no other reason. 'And if—when—I go away again, I'll only have to find someone to take your place.'

Some women would have told him that they would think about it. Some might even have told him to look after his own house and to stuff his three pokey rooms.

Ellie did neither of those things.

She smiled.

Not a smile of triumph, or satisfaction, but a smile that could light up a room. A smile that could recharge a moribund heart. And he found himself taking a step back from what felt like a punch in the chest, a blow as painful as anything he'd felt when she'd fallen on him.

'Can I ask you something?' she asked. He waited. There was no chance that, having made up her mind to it, she wouldn't ask whatever she wanted. 'Whereabouts are the withers?'

'Between the shoulderblades. Of a horse,' he added.

She nodded. 'I thought so. I'll be sure to add liniment to my shopping list.'

Ellie, unable to believe her luck, beat a swift retreat to the safety of her own little self-contained world in the turret, and went straight up to her study, under the conical slate roof. She shooed the cat from the comfort of the 'to-do' basket so that she could add the dentist's reminder to the pile of filing and other stuff awaiting her attention.

Studiously ignoring the large brown envelope, Ellie sat down, letting out a whoosh of air that she hadn't been conscious of holding. 'We've got a reprieve, Millie!' she said, scooping up the local paper and tossing it into the bin.

Millie twitched her tail, annoyed at being disturbed, and settled on the windowsill.

'Don't get sniffy with me, madam. If I'm homeless, so are you, so you'd better not do anything to blot your copybook,' she said, but grinned. Another few months might not make any difference to Ben Faulkner, but it made the world of difference to her, and she had no doubts who to thank for it.

Kitty was a secretary of the old school. All crisp vowels, dark suits and no nonsense. She must have told Ben in no uncertain terms that his sister had made a deal and he must stick to it.

The real mystery was why he found it so hard.

No, the real mystery was why he was alone in this big old house.

Then, since speculation—however pleasing it was to her novelist's imagination to daydream about a good-looking man and what dark secrets might drive him—would, as her great-grandma had been fond of saying, butter no parsnips, she updated her work diary.

This was where she kept a list of the jobs she was booked for, hours worked, a running total of the money she'd earned.

Today, as every morning, she had spent an hour putting the local estate agent's office straight before moving on to the optician's. Then, because it was Friday, she'd shopped for Mrs Williams. After that she'd picked up Daisy Thomas from nursery school and looked after her until her mother returned from the hospital.

That done, she turned to her personal diary—an indulgent, A4-sized leather-covered volume worthy of a novelist. The smooth, fine paper was perfect for spilling out the details of her day, the weird incidents that happened when you were working in other people's homes, for scribbling her little illustrations as she went.

Nothing much so far today. Unlike yesterday, which had been rather too incident-packed, work had been uneventful. Even her trip to the market—frequently the source of amusement—had lacked drama.

All she had to fill the blank day was Rejection Number Eleven. She wrote it down. Underlined it.

She was keeping count so that when her book was a bestseller she could tell the journalists flocking to her door exactly how many people had been dumb enough to turn her down before her genius was recognised. Wouldn't all the rest of them feel really stupid then?

Probably not.

But back to reality, and the lurking presence of that large brown envelope. She doodled a little line drawing of the cat who was once again curled up in the 'to-do' basket.

She drew the little cupcakes with angel wings that she'd baked with Daisy to keep her from worrying about her mother.

Drew a floppy lick of hair that was just like the way Ben Faulkner's hair fell across his forehead.

Now there was a subject that would fill a book.

Dr Benedict Faulkner.

She couldn't believe how rude he'd been yesterday. And yet he'd strapped her up, given her a lift to work, then come and collected her from the library.

More than any girl could ask, in fact—until he'd spoiled it all by implying she was prepared to offer more than a bit of dusting in return for accommodation. Ironic, under the circumstances. At least Kitty had put him straight about that.

Maybe she should write one of those hideous 'true-life' stories that some weekly magazines headlined on their covers. It was no more than he deserved.

I-fell-off-a-ladder-at-work-and-lost-my-job...

Nowhere near sensational enough.

I-fell-off-a-ladder-and-ruined-my-boss's-sex-life...

Better.

I-fell-off-a-ladder-into-my-boss's-arms-and-he-kissed-me...

What? Oh, no...

Writing fairy tales was one thing, but believing in them was something else. And with that thought she stopped putting off the inevitable and tore open the big envelope.

Her book had obviously caught the reader on a really bad day, and instead of just returning it with a pre-printed slip she had decided to tell her exactly what she thought about it. She didn't stint herself, making free with words such as 'clichéd' and 'dated'. For a moment Ellie just sat there, completely stunned, before quickly opening a drawer and pushing the thing out of sight.

She had better things to do than worry about another rejection for her novel.

Mrs Cochrane wanted the names of the ferns in her trough by Monday, and since she knew absolutely nothing about ferns it was going to involve knocking on a total stranger's door and asking. The sooner the better.

Her ring on the doorbell was answered by a call from the rear of the house.

'I'm round the back.'

Ellie found the owner of the voice, an elegant blonde

who could have been anywhere between forty-five and sixty, stretched out on a sofa in a huge old-fashioned conservatory, peering through high-powered binoculars. She didn't get up but, sparing her a momentary glance, said, 'I was expecting someone else.'

'Oh,' Ellie said, slightly disconcerted by this offhand reception, but ploughed ahead. 'Well, I'm sorry to bother you, but I walk past your garden every day and I've been admiring your ferns. I was wondering if you could tell me what they are?'

'You're that girl who's living in Wickham Lodge, aren't you?' the woman said, finally lowering the binoculars and looking at her properly.

'Yes, that's right. I'm house-sitting. At least I was. Now Dr Faulkner's home, I suppose I'm demoted to cleaner.' She offered her hand. 'Ellie March. How d'you do?'

'Morrison. Laura Morrison. I've seen you, cutting the grass.' Then, after a long, assessing look, 'So, Ellie, what do you know about ferns?'

'Absolutely nothing,' she admitted. 'But there's this stone trough at the back of the Lodge where I thought they might just work. The pansies in there certainly don't look happy.'

'They won't. Pansies like the sun. Hate being wet.'

She should certainly know. Her garden was stunning. Flowers spilled over enticing stone paths that wound between herbaceous beds before disappearing behind flowering shrubs. A glimpse of roof suggested a summerhouse tucked away in the trees. And there was an exquisite gothic bird-feeder being mobbed by small birds.

It was all on a much smaller scale than the garden at Wickham Lodge, but it echoed the way—in her imagination—'Lady Gabriella's' garden would look, how

Ben Faulkner's garden would look given sufficient care and attention. Informal, exciting, with hidden places for children to claim as their own.

'There should be some ferns behind the greenhouse,' said Lady Morrison. 'I'd get up and find them for you, but my back's gone into a spasm.'

'Oh, I am sorry. Is there anything I can do?'

'You could pour me a whisky.' Then, before Ellie could query the wisdom of mixing liquor with painkillers, Laura Morrison's eyes narrowed. 'Stand aside,' she hissed, and whipped out a pistol.

Ellie, scarcely able to believe her eyes, just stood there, open-mouthed.

'Out of my way, girl!' she said, taking aim, and Ellie belatedly turned to see what had caused such a reaction. It was Millie, fat little belly hugging the grass, who, having followed her, was now creeping up on one of the bird-feeders.

'No!' she cried, without a thought in her head for the consequences as she leapt to block Laura Morrison's aim.

Something stung her ankle, and as she crumpled in a heap on the floor it crossed her mind that she was having a very bad week for legs.

'I don't believe it,' she declared, more surprised than hurt—shock, no doubt. 'You shot me!'

CHAPTER FIVE

'YOU'VE shot me,' Ellie repeated, unable to quite believe it.

'Don't be stupid, girl.'

'Stupid!' Outraged, Ellie said, 'There's blood running down my leg! See,' she said, pulling up the leg of her cropped trousers, forcing herself to look.

She blinked.

There was no sign of blood. No damage.

'But I felt it...' The sting of something hitting her. The damp trickle. She touched her skin, and sure enough her fingers came away wet—but not with blood. 'It looks like water...'

'It is water,' Laura Morrison said. 'Unless you wet yourself with fright?'

She might have, if she'd had time to be frightened. 'That's a water pistol?'

'Of course it is.' Then, 'Did you really think I had a firearm?'

'Um...yes.'

'Stupid, but brave,' she said.

'No,' Ellie assured her, 'stupid does it.' Then, with

only her pride hurt, she picked herself up, wincing as she put her leg to the ground.

'Did you hurt yourself when you fell?' Laura asked, finally concerned.

'No, I did the knee yesterday, when I was dusting.'

'Dusting? I have to admit that I never saw that as a dangerous pastime.'

'It is when you do it at the top of a ladder.' A colourful array of bruises had emerged overnight to confirm this fact. She wondered if Ben Faulkner had a matching mirror set, left shoulder, right thigh... Best stop right there, she told herself, and tuned back in to Laura Morrison, who was laughing.

'You do live an exciting life. Are you sure something as down-to-earth as gardening is quite your thing?'

'I seem to have the knack of turning the most mundane activity into an adventure,' she said, her own smile a touch wry. Then, as Laura Morrison winced, she forgot her own aches. 'Have you seen a doctor? For your back?'

'For all the good he did. Painkillers and bed-rest was the best he could offer.'

About to suggest that maybe she should do as he'd advised and go to bed, so that she could lie flat, Ellie thought better of it, suspecting that she was not the kind of woman who took kindly to unasked-for advice.

'Could it be tension?' she offered instead. 'My mother's back seizes solid whenever Great-Aunt Jane comes to visit.'

It was possible that an invasion of neighbourhood cats treating her garden as a fast food franchise might have the same effect on Laura Morrison.

'She finds massage helpful,' she continued—her mother occasionally voiced the opinion that she'd been vaccinated with a gramophone needle. 'She's fit for anything after that.'

'Really? Likes a young man giving her a good working over, does she?' Ellie, not normally given to blushing, blushed furiously. Laura's laughter was brought up short by another spasm. 'Good for her. I've got my own young man coming any time now. In fact I thought you were him.'

'Oh.' She'd been teasing. 'I'm sorry to have disappointed you.'

'On the contrary, my dear, you've been thoroughly entertaining. You must come again, when I'm on my feet.' Then, 'Now, go and get those ferns.'

She did as she was told, sorting through dozens of pots before returning with a likely assortment of ferns in a tray and anticipating a botany lecture.

'You've missed the grey and red one,' said Laura, sending her back for it. 'Yes. That should do. Take a look at my planter on the way out and you'll see how to lay them out.'

'What? Oh, you mean these are for me? But I just wanted the names…'

Which roughly translated meant, Oh, bother. I'd rather not… It was information she'd wanted, something she could use in her column, not a do-it-yourself dirt-under-the-fingernails lesson in gardening.

'No point in buying them when these are just sitting around, no use or ornament. You'll find the names on the labels.'

'Well, that's really very generous. Thank you.'

Laura Morrison waved her thanks away. 'Just buy a bell for your cat and we'll call it quits.'

Uh-oh. 'How did you know it was my cat?'

'It's my back that's unreliable, not my eyesight. I've seen you sitting at your window, playing with your computer. And I've seen that cat climbing in through your window.' She touched the binoculars. 'I like to know my enemy.' Before Ellie could answer, there was a ring at the doorbell. 'That'll be Josh. Send him round, will you?' Then, 'Don't let those plants dry out.'

'I won't. I'm really very grateful, Miss Morrison.'

'Laura. Come again soon, Ellie. But leave the cat behind.'

Ben was looking at the text in front of him, but he might as well have had his eyes closed for all the sense he was making of it. He couldn't get Ellie March out of his head. The way she'd kept those huge brown eyes of hers averted as he'd walked into the kitchen, as if by not looking at him she would somehow render herself invisible. As if he might overlook her presence. Forget she was there.

Impossible. If she'd been some quiet, mousy female he would have had no problem with her, but she wasn't either of those things. Even when she wasn't around she still managed to fill the house with her presence. She was there in every gleaming surface, every plumped-up cushion, in a lingering scent that he couldn't put a name to, one that didn't come out of any bottle.

She disturbed the very air, and he'd wanted her out of his house, out of his life, and the sooner the better.

His mistake had been talking to Kitty. Maybe he'd been looking for some salve for his conscience—justification, confirmation of the lack of any formal agreement or contract. It was clear that there was neither, which should have made things easier. Too late, he discovered that it didn't.

With a formal agreement there would have been a measure of equity, protection on both side. It would have given him a get-out clause, a period of notice to be given in writing. She would have had rights and, having acknowledged them, he would have been able to rest easy.

Somehow, this gentlemen's agreement his sister had thought sufficient—and he was quite sure that the lease for her own apartment hadn't been anywhere near as casual—had left him with no choice but to behave like a gentleman.

He might have to live with it, with her. But he didn't have to like it.

As he sat there, work neglected, he gradually became aware of the small sounds of the garden filtering in through the open window. A blackbird in the lilac tree, singing its heart out. Small insects, bees mobbing the wisteria. The softly repeated chink, chink, chink of someone working in the garden with a hoe or a small hand tool.

He closed the window. Returned to his desk. But even when he'd blotted out the sound he could still hear it in his head and, furious at the disturbance, he walked out of the front door, around the house, determined to tell her to stop whatever she was doing, give him some peace.

When, finally, he came across her, bent over the old stone trough by the kitchen door, it was too late to regret the impulse, to wish he'd stayed put. To late to back away. It was a re-run of that moment in the library.

A re-run of his life.

And yet everything was different. The woman was a mess. Her hair tugged back in an elastic band, her temple streaked with dirt. She was wearing cut-offs that

displayed practically every inch of her shapely legs, the
nearest sporting a bruise that mirrored the one on his
thigh—a physical reminder, should he need one, of their
first encounter. She had battered blue pumps with bright
red laces on her feet, and to top it all a blindingly bright
pink crop top clung to her untidily generous curves.

'What are you doing?' he demanded.

Ellie, having made a note of the Latin names of the
ferns—handily printed on plastic labels stuck into the
pots—and despatched them by e-mail to Jennifer
Cochrane, along with a proposal for a feature on the imagi-
native fabric playhouses designed and made by one of the
ladies she cleaned for, had felt the tug of conscience.

Laura Morrison had been kind enough to give her the
ferns. The least she could do was plant them.

It hadn't occurred to her to clear the idea with Ben
Faulkner first. Why would it?

'A neighbour gave me these,' she said, gesturing at
the waiting pots with the trowel. 'Apparently they like
damp shade. Unlike these pansies which, it has to be
faced, are on their last legs.'

When he didn't answer, she glanced over her shoulder.

'They were never happy there,' he agreed. 'Never
thrived.'

His initial irritation had faded into something else,
something that tugged at her heartstrings. The haunted
note she'd caught in his voice was in his eyes, too. But
it wasn't her he was looking at, but the sad, elongated
plants, all stalk and tiny leaves where they'd hunted for
the light. Belatedly, she wondered who had planted them.

Not him—he wouldn't have overreacted that way if
it had been him. Someone he'd cared for, then, she
decided, remembering how she'd kept a potted plant

Sean had bought her, some ghastly purple chrysanthemum, long after it had shrivelled up and died.

'I'm sorry, Ben,' she said, picking them up very carefully, tucking their roots back into the damp soil so that they wouldn't just lie there and die, then easing herself to her feet. 'I'll put them somewhere where they'll be happier,' she said. 'I'll ask Laura. Laura Morrison. She'll know.'

For a moment she thought he was going to tell her to forget it. To turn and walk away.

He didn't.

'You'll need some fresh compost if they're going to survive,' he said, after a moment or two.

'The pansies?'

'The ferns. Possibly something ericaceous. I believe woodland plants prefer an acid environment.'

'Sorry, you lost me right after "compost".'

'I'm just guessing. Someone at the garden centre will know.' Then, 'Do you want to go and fetch some?'

'Compost?' Ellie used the seat of her pants to brush the dirt from her hands. Then, 'Are you offering to take me to the garden centre to pick some up?'

'It comes in sacks. I may be wrong, but I suspect you'd find it difficult to manage on your bike.'

'I wouldn't even try.' Then, 'Maybe we should take Adele's car? It would be a shame to mess up yours. And it'll have more room in the back.'

'How much compost do you imagine you'll need?'

'I don't know. I'm not a gardener.'

'That makes two of us.' He shrugged. 'You may have a point. To be honest, I'm surprised Adele didn't offer you the use of her car as a perk of the job. Or maybe she's not as free with her own possessions as she is with mine.'

'Oh, no! She did offer. I can't drive.'

'Can't?'

'I've tried. Sean tried everything. But I have a problem with making my left hand do one thing while my left leg is doing something else and still looking at the road. He told me there's a word for it.'

'I'm sure he did,' he said, with a fleeting suspicion of something that might have been amusement momentarily transforming his face, offering her a glimpse of a very different Ben Faulkner.

Ellie, who rarely got to out-of-town places such as garden centres, left Ben to get all technical on the subject of compost with one of the staff while she wandered off to marvel over the colours and varieties of the endless trays of bedding plants, wonderful pots, bright new tools.

Ben found her looking at a stainless steel trowel with something approaching lust.

'Ready?' he asked.

'Mmm,' she said, replacing it on the display. 'You know, I could really *get* gardening.'

'If you didn't have the world's most romantic novel to finish.'

'Oh, it's finished. I had rejection number eleven today.'

'Eleven? Is that all? You've got a long way to go to catch up with some of the great writers.'

'I make no claims to greatness,' she said. 'Even so, I don't suppose anyone ever told them they were "clichéd".' She couldn't believe she was telling him that.

'Maybe you should stop trying to imitate Emily Brontë and try writing about your own life?' he suggested. 'That would be different.'

That was why, she thought She could rely on him not

to be sensitive, not to save her feelings by suggesting that agents knew nothing, publishers were blind—a frequent moan at the Writers' Circle.

'Are you all done here?' he asked.

'Yes.' Then, 'No. Can you spare another minute or two?'

'I'm in no hurry.'

She led the way to a corner of the store, where glass-sided pens held baby rabbits and guinea pigs. The warm, musky scent of animals and sawdust took her straight back to her childhood.

'I wondered if they still sold them. My dad used to bring me here when I was little,' she said, bending down to pick up a sleek-coated jet-black baby bunny. 'I wanted a rabbit so much. One just like this,' she said, gently stroking it.

'Why? They don't do anything.'

'They're soft and furry.'

'So are soft toys,' he pointed out, 'and they're much less work.'

'But not warm.' She glanced at Ben. 'Maybe it's a girl thing.' She sighed. 'Poor little things. They're going to spend their lives shut up in tiny little cages, most of them, forgotten after a week or two. Left for Mum to clean out and feed.'

'Stupid Mum for buying it in the first place.'

She turned to glance at him. 'Oh, come on. Didn't you bug your mother for a pet, Ben?'

'My mother died when I was very young.'

Oh… Oh… 'I'm so sorry.'

'Why?' Then, not waiting for her answer, to hear meaningless words that he'd no doubt heard a hundred times before, he shook his head. 'Dogs,' he said. 'We always had dogs.'

'I was never allowed a dog.'

'Given the choice,' he said, 'I'd have opted for a mother.'

Damn! He'd finally managed to bring her nonsense to a halt, shut her up. But, confronted by her stricken face, he wished he'd held his tongue.

'My father had a black Labrador,' he said, in a bid to wipe that look from her eyes. 'I had a golden retriever and an assortment of mongrels. And there was a red setter, too, that Adele brought home from a rescue centre. You put me in mind of her.'

'Adele?'

'The setter.'

Her brows dived in a puzzled frown. 'But I don't have red hair.'

'Then it must be the temperament. Boisterous. Feather-brained. Never knows when to stop.'

'Feather-brained?'

She had the same eyes, too. Large, expressive, the colour of warm treacle. Nothing was hidden. Every thought laid bare.

'That's a little harsh,' she said. Then, having thought about it for a moment, she twitched her shoulder in the smallest of shrugs and said, 'Or maybe not.' Then, 'No cats, rabbits, guinea pigs, hamsters?' she pressed, as if determined on proving his point. 'What about mice? Surely you had mice? *All* boys have mice.'

'Then you've answered your own question, haven't you? Are you done here?' he asked, with a gesture at the pens.

'Yes.' She put the rabbit back. Stood watching it for a moment. 'I shouldn't have come over here,' she said with a sigh, as they headed for the checkout. 'It was okay when I was a kid. It never occurred to me to empathise with a rabbit when I was six. Twenty years on, I won't be able to stop thinking about him.'

They had almost reached the checkout when she stopped. 'Hold on.'

'Ellie!' he warned.

'I won't be a minute,' she called back. True to her word, she returned a few moments later with a large terracotta pot shaped like an old-fashioned flowerpot. 'I'll take this, too,' she said.

'Thank heavens for that. I was afraid you'd gone back for the rabbit,' he said, as she put it on the trolley.

'Listen, feather-brained I may be. Plain stupid I'm not.' She fished her purse out of her bag and took out a twenty-pound note.

'Put your money away, Ellie.'

'Oh, but—'

'My trough. I buy the compost.'

'But the pot...'

'Will be in my garden.'

'I might want to take it when I leave.'

'Don't tease me with empty threats. We both know you're not going anywhere.' Then, 'It's up to you, Ellie, but if you want to pay for it, you're going to have to come back and fetch it on your bike.'

She lifted it onto the counter without another word. Mouth zipped. Restraint personified.

'Damn it!'

'What?' she asked, startled, as he put the pot back on the trolley and pulled out of the queue. 'What did I do?'

Nothing. She didn't have to *do* anything. She was exactly like that damn setter; she wore her heart in her eyes. Right now, while the rest of her face was doing its best to be on its best behaviour, they betrayed her.

'Go and get the blasted rabbit!'

Delight and disappointment chased each other over her face, warring for supremacy. 'I can't.'

'Can't?'

'It's not that easy.' Seeing his obvious bafflement, she said, 'It's my turn to play the responsible mother, Ben. Where will it live?'

'They sell those flat-pack A-frame animal houses here, don't they?'

'Yes.' She swallowed. 'They do.' Her shoulders twitched in another little shrug.

'But?'

'But he'll need a wire enclosure so he has somewhere to run.'

He wasn't being pushed to provide a rabbit palace. Ellie was giving him a chance to have second thoughts, he realised. Back off. Common sense suggested that it would be the wise option.

'There's a DIY place next door,' he said. 'We can call in and pick up some posts and chicken wire.'

'Do you mean that?'

Yes. No. 'I wouldn't have said it if I didn't mean it.'

She shook her head. 'This is weird. I don't know what to say.'

'Is that a fact?' An unbidden smile broke out, reaching every corner of his face. 'And all it took was a rabbit? Unbelievable!'

Ellie's laugh was a joyous sound. 'You won't regret it,' she promised, speech not a problem after all, apparently.

'Oh, I'm sure I will,' he warned. 'I'd advise you not to waste any time.'

'I'll, um, need a hand. With the hutch. And stuff.'

'I'll sort out the hutch. You sort out the "stuff".'

'Something tall enough,' she insisted. 'Rabbits need to be able to keep their ears upright.'

'You're kidding?'

'No! I'm buying his house and I want him to have plenty of room.' She suddenly caught on to the fact that *he* was kidding and pulled a face. 'And he'll need straw. And sawdust.'

How had he seen only the soft eyes, missed that determined chin? How on earth did he come to be buying rabbit bedding instead of sitting in the peace of his study, deciphering a recently discovered early form of Devanagari? How had he somehow committed himself to building a rabbit run for a woman who had no right to be living in his house in the first place?

'It's a good thing we brought Adele's car,' she said, as he picked up a vacuum-packed bale of straw. 'We'd never have got all this into your sports car.'

'My mistake,' he said.

'You don't mean that,' she said, her eyes sparkling. 'You put on a good act, Ben, but you're not the grouch you pretend to be.'

'I am,' he said to her retreating back. 'Truly.' She just waved his words away without even turning around.

When she returned, she had a cardboard carrying box in each hand. Behind her was an assistant, carrying food, feeders, a water container. 'Rabbits are gregarious creatures,' she said, undeterred by his horrified expression. 'Roger will need company.'

'Not another rabbit,' he said, with what he hoped was unarguable firmness.

'Oh, please. I'm not that dumb.' He gave her a look

that suggested the jury was out on that one. 'Really. This,' she said, holding up the smaller box, 'is Nigel. He's a guinea pig. And you,' she said, standing on tiptoe and, before he realised what was coming, kissing his cheek, 'are a very kind man.'

For a moment, with both hands full, she wobbled, and he reached out to steady her, a hand on each arm. Her skin was golden, silky smooth, warm to his palms, her eyes, mouth, her entire face lit up like a kid on her birthday. For a moment he longed to kiss her laughing mouth, tap into that simple pleasure in every moment well lived.

How had she managed that? Turned her life around from such tragedy to such joy?

Ben, wearing jeans so soft and thin with wear that the cloth had split under the strain to expose a glimpse of knee and thigh, was swinging a mallet to hammer posts into a shady patch of lawn. Ellie, bringing him coffee, paused for moment on the edge of the lawn to indulge herself in the pleasure of watching him.

'Can I do anything to help?' she asked, as he stopped, straightened, wiped his forehead on the sleeve of his T-shirt and glanced at her, apparently sensing her presence despite the fact that she'd done nothing to attract his attention.

'I think you've done quite enough for one day.'

'Me? This was your idea.'

'Of course it was. When I offered to run you to the garden centre for a bag of compost, it was my firm intention to return with a menagerie.'

'We're very grateful.'

'We?'

'Roger, Nigel and me.' Then, 'Actually, we all think you should get a dog. For yourself.'

'The cat doesn't have a say in this?' He stopped her before she could answer, took the mug she was offering him, and said, 'No dog.' Then, 'It's possible I'll be returning to Kirbeckistan in the near future.'

'I'll be here to take care of it.' Then, 'It'll be here to take care of me.'

'In other words *you* want a dog.'

'The house would like a dog.'

'No dog.'

'Okay,' she said, turning away, walking back to the house.

'I mean it, Ellie.'

She lifted a hand in acknowledgement. He was not reassured.

CHAPTER SIX

A SECOND batch of letters had arrived from the *Milady* offices, and Ellie spent an entire afternoon answering them, using the heavy cream stationery supplied for this purpose.

Her column rambled over her impressions of the garden centre, described the small black rabbit and the honey-coloured guinea pig that had joined the family menagerie. How 'Daddy' had built a fox-proof house for them—with the hindrance of the children, who had been eager to help—and an extensive run on the shady side of the daisy-strewn lawn.

She drew little sketches of both rabbit and guinea pig, as well as her giant flowerpot overflowing with pansies. Under advice from Laura, she'd replanted the ones she'd dug up, trimmed off the lank growth and stood them in some semi-shade where, maybe, with a bit of luck, they'd eventually match her imagination.

Mrs Cochrane had offered reserved approval, said that a staff reporter was already working on a photo feature on the playhouses, and made it clear that next month she wanted *food*.

Ellie was a bit miffed about the feature, and as for

food—well, for heaven's sake, it was *her* life she was writing about. When food happened, she'd write about it.

Then, realistically, she decided that probably wasn't going to work. Food didn't happen in her life. She was going to have to make an effort. Maybe she could cook something for Ben. A special thank-you. There would be some point to that.

Enthused, she asked one of her clients—a serious cook—for advice. Armed with a menu and a shopping list, she shopped on the way home. Once there, she updated her diary, and then dug out her rejected book.

She'd been putting off sending it to the next name on her list. Was there any point? Maybe Ben was right. Instead of emulating her idols, maybe she should be writing what she knew. Feather-brained girl doing the unpleasant jobs that the well-heeled, the useless—that would be the men—or just plain desperate, were prepared to pay someone else to do.

Like that would sell, she thought. Then began to leaf back through her diary, reliving some of the blush-making incidents, the stuff that made her laugh out loud, the horrors.

Maybe there was something. Leaving it to stew in the back of her mind, she went out to take Roger and Nigel a carrot and a few dandelion leaves. Then, because in the war between the grass and the dandelions the dandelions were winning, she got out the ride-on mower. Ben had said to leave it, that he'd do it, but there was something about doing mindless, repetitive jobs that untangled her thoughts, made everything seem simpler.

And just lately things had become very complicated. *Milady*. Ben. Ben. *Milady*. Ben…

She'd been working for about twenty minutes when

Would you like to read Harlequin Romance® novels with larger print?

Larger Print Editions

GET 2 FREE LARGER PRINT BOOKS!

Harlequin Romance® novels are now available in a larger print edition! These books are complete and unabridged, but the type is larger, so it's easier on your eyes.

YES! Please send me 2 FREE *Harlequin Romance* novels in the larger print format and 2 FREE mystery gifts! I understand I am under no obligation to purchase any books, as explained on the back of this card.

386 HDL ELX3   186 HDL ELZ3

FIRST NAME   LAST NAME

ADDRESS

APT #   CITY

STATE/PROV.   ZIP/POSTAL CODE

Order online at:
www.eHarlequin.com

HLP-R-05/07

The Harlequin Reader Service® — Here's How It Works:

Accepting your 2 free Harlequin Romance® larger print books and 2 free gifts places you under no obligation to buy anything. You may keep the books and gifts and return the shipping statement marked "cancel." If you do not cancel, about a month later we'll send you 6 additional Harlequin Romance larger print books and bill you just $3.82 each in the U.S. or $4.30 each in Canada, plus 25¢ shipping & handling per book and applicable taxes if any.* That's the complete price and — compared to cover prices of $4.50 each in the U.S. and $5.25 each in Canada — it's quite a bargain! You may cancel at any time, but if you choose to continue, every month we'll send you 6 more books, which you may either purchase at the discount price or return to us and cancel your subscription.

*Terms and prices subject to change without notice. Sales tax applicable in N.Y. Canadian residents will be charged applicable provincial taxes and GST. All orders subject to approval. Credit or debit balances in a customer's account(s) may be offset by any other outstanding balance owed by or to the customer. Please allow 4 to 6 weeks for delivery.

You'll get 2 FREE mystery gifts along with your 2 FREE books!

If offer card is missing write to: Harlequin Reader Service, 3010 Walden Ave., P.O. Box 1867, Buffalo, NY 14240-1867.

BUSINESS REPLY MAIL
FIRST-CLASS MAIL   PERMIT NO. 717-003   BUFFALO, NY

POSTAGE WILL BE PAID BY ADDRESSEE

HARLEQUIN READER SERVICE
3010 WALDEN AVE
PO BOX 1867
BUFFALO NY 14240-9952

NO POSTAGE
NECESSARY
IF MAILED
IN THE
UNITED STATES

she turned and saw one of her complications walking round the corner of the house. He'd gone into the university first thing that morning, and for a moment she was transfixed by how utterly gorgeous he looked in a dark shirt, well-cut stone-coloured trousers, his hair flopping untidily over his forehead.

'Stop!'

Belatedly realising that she was running out of lawn, she hunted for the brake with her foot, then, when she couldn't find it, looked down.

'What the hell do you think you're doing?'

That was promising. The last time he'd asked that, Roger and Nigel had moved in. Maybe this was going to be a good day for some poor mutt who needed a home...

'What's up, Doc?' she asked, as she finally managed to bring the thing to a halt before she cut a swathe through a bed filled with a riot of perennials.

Ben, who'd had to move sharply to avoid being mown down, ignored the Bugs Bunny routine and said, 'Do you think this is a good idea?'

'Excuse me?'

'You've just given me a very close demonstration of your lack of hand/eye co-ordination skills.'

She grinned up at him. 'Aw, shucks. I never touched you.'

True. But somehow the way she said it made it a matter for regret rather than congratulation.

'You're a menace.'

'Relax. I'm cutting grass, not driving round the ring-road. There's no one to bump into—well, no one but you, and you're pretty nifty on your feet when you see the danger coming.'

Not nearly nifty enough, he thought, or he wouldn't

be stuck with Ellie March and her growing menagerie as his own personal live-in torment.

'What is your sport?' she asked.

'I really think you should leave this to me, Ellie,' he replied, ignoring her attempt to change the subject.

'I'll bet it's rugby. On the wing, right?'

'Off the mower. Now.'

'Oh, I get it.' She sat back. 'This is a "boy's toy".' She gestured broadly at the machine she was sitting astride. 'Girls are supposed to stick to the boring stuff, like sweeping up the bits of grass that get sprayed onto the path.' She shook her head. 'My dad used to be just the same. Kept all the good stuff to do himself, then wondered why we didn't want to play.' With that, she swung one leg high over the steering wheel, offering a heart-stopping display of leg, before sliding off the seat. 'I'm nearly done, anyway. There's just that bit down there by the treehouse.'

He looked in the direction of the old oak. 'What tree-house? There was never a treehouse.'

'Wasn't there?' Her face was flushed pink by the sun, but even so he could have sworn she blushed. 'Well, there should have been. The way the branches spread out to make the perfect platform is just begging for one. I can't believe your dad didn't build you some kind of den up there when you were a kid.'

'My father was in his fifties when I was born. Climbing trees was a bit beyond him by the time I was old enough to want such a thing.'

'Oh, right. I didn't think—'

'I was right about you, Ellie. You're exactly like Adele's idiotic red setter. You just leap in, say the first thing that comes into your head, and you don't know when to quit.'

'Some people think that's a good quality,' she said, then added, 'The not quitting thing.'

'Clearly they haven't been on the receiving end of one of your inquisitions.' Then, in an attempt to turn the tables, he said, 'What about you?'

'Me? You want to know about my family? Mum's a great cook, she's a member of the Women's Institute, helps out at a charity shop three times a week. Dad is a civil servant. Taxes.' She shook her head. 'We don't talk about that outside the family. My sister takes after him. You'd like her. She's the sensible one with brains—'

'I'm not interested in them. I said I'd do this when I got home, so why are you out here cutting my grass when you should be devoting all your time to writing? That *is* what this alternative lifestyle is in aid of? The reason you gave up your legitimate career? Your life? So that you can write?'

'I needed thinking time, and I can think and mow the lawn at the same time,' she said. 'And I haven't given up my life.'

'No? I share a house with you, and I haven't seen any signs of one. When was the last time you went out on a date?'

'Good question,' she said without hesitation. 'When did you?' Then, before he could answer, 'Do you want to come to dinner tonight? I'm trying out a recipe and I need someone who'll give me an honest opinion. I know I can rely on you for that.'

'You're evading the question.'

'And you aren't?' she demanded. 'I'm not ready to date. What's your excuse?'

For a moment neither of them spoke, giving him

plenty of time to regret that he'd followed the sound of the mower. To wish that he'd gone straight inside.

'I haven't given up my life, Doc, I'm going for it.' She stood, hands on hips, looking as if she was about to take on the world. 'I've done all the sensible stuff, made all the compromises. Never again.'

'You're taking the balloon ride?'

'As far as hot air and a following wind will take me.'

'You're sure you're not just running away?'

She stared at him, shocked for a moment into silence. Then, 'No!'

'No?' He wasn't sure where that thought had come from, except suddenly he wasn't as convinced by this cheerful, go-for-it exterior as he should be. Ellie had suffered a terrible loss, and instead of rebuilding her life she appeared to be running blindly into the future, doing her best to escape it. 'So why, when you decided to fly, didn't you go back to your first love and enrol in art school?'

She took a breath as if to speak. Didn't. Couldn't. Opened her mouth. Closed it.

'Well?' he pressed, certain now in every fibre of his being that he'd got beneath the outer shell to touch something soft, raw at her centre.

'It was too late,' she finally managed. Her arms had dropped to her sides and she was no longer quite as self-assured, in-your-face-confident. 'I'm a different person.'

'People don't change.'

'Maybe I didn't want it badly enough in the first place.'

'Maybe,' he said, 'you were always too scared to go for it. Maybe that's why you didn't push for it in the first place. Override your father's objections.'

Her father? When had she said it was her father

who'd talked her out of it? She shook her head. It didn't matter.

'What's this? Psychology Central? You're not exactly living life to the full yourself. You get plenty of invitations. I empty the bin you toss them in. So who messed up your life, Doc?'

And it was his turn to do the fish impression.

She shook her head, just once, said, 'Life isn't a rehearsal, it's one long first night.'

'Maybe I don't like the script.'

'Then change it. You get dumped on the stage, but the moves are up to you. The important thing is to keep moving.'

Then, as if to show him how it was done, she turned and began to walk away from him. The cut-offs were the same ones she'd worn on the day they went to the garden centre, clinging to her hips, accentuating her bottom which, as she walked, swung in the opposite direction to her heavy dark ponytail. The effect was hypnotic.

'Natasha,' he called after her. Anything to stop that swaying. Anything to stop her from walking away. 'Her name was Natasha.'

It worked. She stopped, turned.

No. That was no better. Now, instead of her bottom, he had a full frontal of her heart-stopping bosom, hugged by a close-fitting vest top that swooped low enough to offer a promise of the delights it concealed. He'd caught more than a glimpse that night he'd taken her to the Assembly Rooms when, oblivious of his presence, she pulled off her top to display the kind of bra that had caused traffic chaos when an equally well-endowed model had displayed one on sixty feet of roadside hoarding.

He'd never been turned on by the too obvious sexuality of wide hips, a generous bosom, an old-fashioned waist, but there had been no doubting the effect Ellie's body had had on him that night.

Or now.

And he kept on inflicting it on himself. While his mind was determined on one course, his body just kept walking into trouble. It was walking into trouble now, he knew, as he took a step towards her.

'She was tall, fair, slender, always perfectly dressed, never a hair out of place,' he said, as if by conjuring up Tasha's pristine pale gold image he could somehow protect himself from a sensual clamour that responded so insistently to Ellie March. 'She spoke ten languages fluently, another seven well enough to carry on a conversation. She was perfection, and I loved her.' He stopped six inches from Ellie. Near enough to smell the grass where tiny pieces of it clung to skin damp with the heat. Near enough to feel the warmth of her body.

'Past tense, Ben?' she asked, her eyes softening, her voice catching in her throat.

'Only in relation to my life.' She waited. For a woman who had a runaway mouth, she understood the power of silence. 'She was offered a job at the highest level of the United Nations.'

'And she took it?'

He felt rather than heard her sharp intake of breath. Having anticipated some great personal tragedy to equal her own desperate loss, she was shocked by this banal story of raw ambition overriding emotion. No story there for her imagination to get to grips with. No passion. Quite the reverse.

'No,' she said, answering her own question. 'If she'd

grabbed for it, walked away, you'd have got over her. You encouraged her to go, didn't you? Made the sacrifice?' She nodded, able to understand that. 'Yes,' she said. 'That's love.'

'No,' he said, 'that's pragmatism. You see a look in a person's eyes, Ellie, and you know, even while she's telling you that it's nothing, even while you're clinging to that, trying to block out reality, that it's over. That you've already lost. One way or another she was going to leave. It was the life she was made for, and I didn't want her to feel guilty about grabbing for it.'

'Pragmatism. Love. They're just words. It's the motivation that counts. The feeling that drives the action.' She paused, as if to catch her breath. 'And now I'm here, in her place, doing the things she'd be doing. Bringing it all back.'

'Yes,' he said, because to lie would be pointless. Then, because strands of dark hair were clinging to her cheek, because she was pink from the sun, because she worried about rabbits instead of world affairs, wrote silly romances rather than reports of world-changing significance, he added, 'And no.' He took her hand, turning it over, looking at her fingers, stained with green. 'You are not perfect.'

'No, I'm a scruffy feather-brain who's ten pounds overweight, has no career prospects and...and can only speak five languages.'

'Five?'

'I can count to ten in French, Italian, German and Welsh,' she said.

'Welsh?'

'*Un, dau, tri, pedwr, pump...* Didn't I mention that my great-grandma was Welsh?'

'If you did I missed it. But are you sure you can count all the way to ten? I only make that four languages.'

She smiled. 'Oh, I can do it in English, too.'

Ben heard himself laughing. What had Ellie said? It didn't matter what you did so long as you did something. And on an impulse he turned his hand so that it was grasping hers. Reaching for the lifeline that she'd tossed him.

'About those invitations. I've been invited to a wedding on Saturday—one that I really can't avoid. Could you bear to come with me?' Then, when she didn't immediately answer, 'That is if you aren't already booked to attend in a professional capacity?'

She shook her head. 'I don't do weddings.'

'Oh, no. It must be…difficult.'

'Horrendous. I always find myself offering champagne to someone who was in the same year as me who's now a rising media star or, worse, is marrying one.'

He knew he was supposed to laugh, but he discovered that he couldn't quite manage it. Couldn't quite decide whether her flippant humour was courage in the face of personal tragedy or refusal to confront the pain. Suspected it might just be the latter.

'This one is in London. My cousin, a contemporary of Adele's, is getting married for the second time. I have to attend on Addy's behalf. The groom is a stockbroker, apparently, so you should be safe enough.' He waited. 'If I go on my own I'll stand out like a sore thumb. Everyone will think I'm either a closet gay or a sad bastard who can't rustle up a partner.'

'Oh, right. You want me to ride shotgun. Fend off the matchmaking aunts.' A shadow briefly crossed her face. 'Enough said. There's just one condition.'

'I'm listening.'

'I meant what I said about you trying out my cooking this evening. Just a mouthful.' Her smile, usually so confident, was unexpectedly diffident.

'It sounds like a win/win deal to me.'

'Wait until you've tasted it before you congratulate yourself. My culinary skills are somewhat limited.'

'I'll risk it. I can pick your brains for a suitable wedding present for the couple who have everything.'

'Oh, no problem. Buy them a goat.'

'A *what*?'

'You said it. They're not spring chickens, and presumably they've both been married before, so they'll have everything they need for their home.'

'Er, yes?'

'So buy a goat, or some tools, or a share in a mango plantation in their name for some Third World family who aren't so fortunate. If nothing else it will give them something to talk about at dinner parties.'

'Where on earth did you come up with an idea like that?'

'Maybe I'm brighter than I look,' she said. Then she shrugged. 'Or maybe I read it in a magazine. I'll find you the website address. You can check it out for yourself.'

A wedding? Ellie stripped off the grass-stained clothes she'd been wearing—nothing elegant or perfect about them—and then turned to look at herself in the mirror.

Not tall. Not fair. Definitely not slender, she thought, pinching the excess at her waist.

She pulled off the band holding her hair in a ponytail and it fell in an untidy mess around her shoulders. Not even a hint of Lady Gabriella, let alone the fabulous and perfect Natasha with her seventeen languages—she was bound to be fluent in all of them by now. Just an over-abundance of Ellie March.

What on earth was she going to wear to a posh London wedding? What would Lady G wear?

She pulled a face. She wasn't even going there. Ben had invited her and that was who he would get. Not her pretend alter ego, and definitely not a second-class Natasha.

Through the open window she heard the mower start up and couldn't help looking out.

Ben had changed into a pair of shorts and a T-shirt. He had fabulous legs, she thought. Not white pasty things that had never seen the sun, but the well-muscled legs of a sportsman, with a sheen of fair hair that glinted in the evening sun.

She drew back as he turned the machine, flexed her hand, feeling again that moment when he'd caught it, turned it into his, held it palm to palm in his and she'd felt a shiver of heat, shocking in its urgency, drive deep into her body.

She'd desired him, wanted him—not in that mean-ingless, fancying-a-good-looking-bloke way that she joked about with Sue, not just physically, but totally, in a way that she'd never thought possible again.

No. It was more than that.

With Sean it had been different. She'd known him all her life. Fought with him in primary school, assidu-ously ignored him when she was ten and eleven and twelve. And then at thirteen he'd smiled at her, and she'd blushed, and then he'd blushed, and after that it had always been Ellie-and-Sean.

They'd done their homework together, gone to the school disco, shared their first kiss, fumbled through their first sexual encounter together, done everything together for the first and last time.

They'd never been parted.

She'd felt safe with him. Had known that he'd never do anything to hurt her.

Except die.

This was different.

Something had been driving her today. Some restless, reckless need to provoke Ben, make him notice her, make him look at her, and she'd stirred him up like a fool poking a stick in a wasp nest.

She hadn't expected him to come right back at her, daring to suggest she was running away from her past rather than grabbing for the future she wanted.

As if.

Well, she'd told him, and then she'd walked away. Easy.

Except he didn't understand the rules. He'd come after her and done the one thing she couldn't ignore. He'd asked for her help.

Nothing difficult. Just go with him to a family wedding. It wasn't the invitation that was a problem. Or even that it was a wedding. Okay, so maybe she'd shed a tear for herself, but she wouldn't be alone.

It was the fact that for Ben it would be duty, nothing more. While for her...

She swallowed, suddenly scared.

It had been so long, more than three years since Sean had died, and there had been no one since. Flirting, yes, but only in a jokey way with men she knew, who were safe, who understood that she didn't mean anything. Wouldn't call her on it because they knew that she had always belonged, would always belong, to Sean.

Somehow, though, Ben Faulkner had slipped beneath her defences. When had that happened?

She switched on the shower, stepped under the water and let the hot water pour over her, scrubbing at the green stains on her fingers, scrubbing her nails, shampooing her hair as if she could somehow clean him from her pores.

It didn't work.

When eventually she stepped from the shower, wrapped a towel around her, tucking it in above her breasts, wrapped another around her hair, she could still feel her hand in his.

Feel the callused roughness from where he'd climbed out of Kirbeckistan. The scars.

Feel the electric charge of his skin against hers, an answering flutter deep in her womb. A sensation that excited her, stirred her, made her long to reach out for something dangerous, something that scared her witless.

Because Ben Faulkner was not like Sean March. If she allowed herself to fall in love with him, he'd hurt her in ways she couldn't begin to imagine—because he'd never love her back.

She swallowed, sat down on the bathroom stool, leaned forward and tugged on the towel so that it hung down over her face.

If?

Too late for if. Too late from the moment she'd lain against him as she'd caught her breath, feeling the beat of his heart. Too late from her first 'idiot'.

It was the first word she'd said to Sean when, five years old, he'd knocked her flying as he'd raced into school one morning. After that, no matter how they'd ignored one another, there had always been a consciousness between them, an awareness of the other.

They'd kept their distance. Scowled. Sniped. Mocked. Circled each other until one day they'd come face to face, alone in a corridor. And, with no one else there to see, he'd smiled at her.

'Sean?' she whispered desperately. 'Where are you?'

CHAPTER SEVEN

BEN, despite every intention of staying well away from the kitchen, couldn't settle. He'd finished cutting the grass, put away the mower. Taken a shower. And then, somehow, he found himself standing in the kitchen doorway, watching Ellie as she chopped onions. She said nothing, did nothing to suggest she knew he was there.

She didn't have to.

There was an awareness between them, something palpable in the air when she was home, that seemed to fill the house. An echoing hollowness about it when she wasn't there, like a room without a carpet.

His first reaction to that had been a how-dare-she? anger. It wasn't her place. She didn't fit. Wasn't right. Natasha had been an expert in the minimalist Japanese style of flower arranging. Ellie favoured the infant school nature table style of floral art. She just stuffed anything she fancied in a jug. Leaves, daisies, even dandelions for heaven's sake.

The way she draped stuff about the place, disguising the wear, softening the edges.

He'd held his tongue, well aware that the more time he spent with her, the harder she became to ignore.

Witness the arrival of Roger and Nigel. She just drew him in, involved him, made him laugh…

'Can I do anything to help?' he asked.

'Just taste the finished dish,' Ellie said, not looking at him, but instead concentrating on chopping the onions to add to an already promising array of ingredients.

'So what are you cooking?' he asked, ignoring her discouraging tone, helping himself to a beer from the fridge and, with the door still open, turning to her. 'Can I get you something?'

'No, thank you.'

He shrugged, let it go, leaned his hip against the table as he snapped the top, took a drink, helped himself to a couple of shelled pistachio nuts from a dish. 'It looks interesting,' he said, refusing to be dismissed. It was, after all, his kitchen.

She flickered a glance in his direction. 'Could you please go away? This is going to be difficult enough without an audience.' Then, 'Stop that,' she said, slapping his hand with the back of her broad-bladed knife as he took another dip in the nuts. 'Everything has been weighed.'

'Chicken, nuts, spices, baby onions.' He picked up a small dish with a few threads of something red in it. 'Is this saffron?'

'Yes.' She sighed, stopped chopping and, clearly hoping that if she satisfied his curiosity he'd leave her in peace, said, 'It's a Moroccan dish. That lot over there—' she pointed with the knife '—is going to be couscous with herbs and nuts and pomegranate.' She glowered at him as he took another nut. 'Assuming there are any nuts left.'

'I won't eat them all,' he assured her.

She shook her head. 'Oh, go on. You might as well enjoy them. I'll probably ruin the whole thing anyway.'

'Nonsense. What are you going to do with the chicken?'

'The plan is to make a tajine of chicken, caramelised onion and pear.'

He scarcely hesitated before he said, 'That sounds interesting.'

'"Interesting". Good word.' She still didn't look at him, just lifted one shoulder in an awkward little shrug. 'One of the women I clean for suggested it. She even loaned me her recipe book. She said the important thing was to keep it simple…'

'This is her idea of simple?'

'She said that even a fool could make it. I didn't like to tell her that my sole experience of planning a meal consisted of choosing a topping for my pizza.'

'Well, that's an art,' he said, wondering what it was about cooking that she found so stressful. 'There's the vexed question of anchovies for a start.'

'Oh, please!' she said, seizing on this distraction. 'You have to have anchovies.'

'Of course you do.'

Now, he thought. Now smile.

'And for pudding?' he pressed, when she didn't.

'Oh, no problem. Lemon tart, crème brûlée, a chocolate roulade.'

'Three?'

'I wanted to see which went best.'

'Right,' he said. Then, 'And we're going to eat tonight?'

'Relax. They're in the fridge.'

'They are?' He hadn't noticed the scent of baking, the inevitable mess that quantity of cooking would entail.

He turned and opened the fridge door again. True enough, three perfectly prepared puddings were sitting out of harm's way on the top shelf. 'They look good.'

'Baking is serious cookery,' she said. Then she sniffed, and he realised that the reason she wasn't looking at him was because she'd been crying. 'Actually, I bought them.'

Well, yes. Obviously.

'Hey, all the best hostesses buy their puddings.'

'They do?' She sniffed again, and he didn't think it was because she couldn't handle a sponge cake.

'Are you okay, Ellie?'

'Fine,' she said. She coaxed the smile into life, looked at him. 'Just a touch of hay fever.'

'Right,' he said, unconvinced. 'Is that recent?'

'Sorry?'

'The hay fever. You didn't seem to have a problem when you were cutting the grass.'

'Oh, no. It must be the onions, then.'

The onions might have set her off again, but, unless she was seriously allergic to them, the puffiness of her eyes, the redness of her nose, suggested that the tears had been flowing for some time. Maybe asking her to go to Emma's wedding with him hadn't been such a great idea—which was a shame because, against all the odds, he was now rather looking forward to it.

'So,' he said, with a gesture at the table, 'what's all this in aid of?' She looked at him fast enough then, those big brown eyes startled wide. Her cheeks almost as pink as her nose. 'You said you're trying this out. I assumed there must be some big occasion coming up.'

'Oh…'

She continued chopping the onion, and he winced as the blade narrowly missed her finger.

'Here. Let me.'

He took it from her and finished the job.

'So?' he asked.

'Yes. Big occasion. It's, um, my sister's birthday in a couple of weeks. I thought I'd cook a meal for her and her friends.'

'And this is the dress rehearsal?'

'Right,' she said, and this time the smile was more of relief rather than any pleasurable anticipation of a family party.

Relief that he'd bought the excuse?

Could straightforward, look-you-in-the-eye-and-give-it-to-you-straight Ellie March be telling him a big fat fib? A blush that competed with her nose suggested that she was, but why? What was the big deal about cooking some special meal? What was she trying to hide?

Unless…

He looked at her. She couldn't meet his gaze, which was totally out of character.

Unless the party was an excuse to cover the fact that she was doing it for him. Which would explain the blushes…

He scooped the onions into a waiting dish.

'Anything else?' he asked.

She shook her head. 'Maybe you'd prefer to miss the main course and go straight to the pudding?'

'Why would I want to do that?'

'Risk aversion?' she offered. 'I'm more at home with a tin of polish than a bottle of olive oil.'

'Nonsense. Between us we can beat this.'

'You can cook?'

'I can read,' he said, wiping his hands and taking the glossy cookery book from its stand. 'How hard can it be?'

Ten minutes later the onions were sizzling in the pan

and Ellie, stirring them carefully while they softened, decided that it wasn't hard at all.

'Ready?'

'Ready,' she said, then added each of the spices as Ben, reading from the recipe, handed them to her.

Then he added the chicken, taking charge when it started to catch. 'Gently does it,' he said, snatching the pan from the heat, turning it down, then returning the pan to her so that she could brown it all over. 'Didn't you learn this at your mother's knee?' he asked.

'No. My sister did all that stuff. I was considered a liability in the kitchen.'

'Hence the need to impress her? Your sister?'

'Pathetic,' she agreed. And she wasn't just referring to her feelings of inferiority.

Why didn't she just tell him the truth? Get it out into the open. Be honest with him. How hard could it be?

The thing is, Ben, I've used your house, your garden, and now, infinitely worse, I've used you to break into print. This meal is so that I can write a convincing portrayal of an al fresco *supper with friends— our friends…*

How would that sound?

Amusing? Opportunistic? Exploitative?

How would she feel if the shoes were on the other feet?

She added the water, covered the pan and turned it down to simmer, turned to him. 'Now what?'

He shook his head. 'That's it for fifteen minutes.'

'It's that easy?'

'Apparently.' Then, checking the recipe, 'Oh, no. Now you have to cover the couscous with boiling water and leave it for fifteen minutes—'

'I think I can handle that.'

'And when that's done we have to add the baby onions to the stew.'

'Stew!' She turned on him, arms akimbo. 'Wash your mouth out, Ben Faulkner. This isn't a stew!'

He laughed. 'Quite right. Sorry, ma'am. Do you want to come down the cellar and help me choose a bottle?'

The cellar. He had to be joking…

'Of mouthwash?'

'I think I can do a little better than that. My father was a wine dealer.'

'Really?' She'd assumed Ben came from a long line of academics.

'Don't tell me you've never seen it? Isn't it part of your duties as house-sitter to inspect every part of the house for potential problems at least once a week?'

'Spiders? Cobwebs?' She couldn't quite control the little shiver that betrayed her. 'I don't think so.'

He regarded her with something like amusement. 'Do I detect just the hint of a phobia?'

'A hint? Please. Do I do anything by halves?' she asked, doing her best to smile back. 'Imagine, if you can, a full-blown case of the screaming habdabs and you'll be close.'

'I'll take that as a no, then, shall I?'

'You get the wine; I'll organise the table.'

A few minutes later he found her in a sheltered walled corner of the courtyard that held the last rays of the sun. He was carrying two glasses of white wine and he handed one to her, looking thoughtfully at the table, laid with a cloth, napkins, silver, a tealight candle in a fancy holder.

'You've gone to a lot of trouble just for a "taste",' he said.

It was true. She had. She'd tried to write about the food without actually going to the bother of cooking it. She just couldn't get the feeling right. She needed to smell the onions and spices cooking, taste them. Feel the dusk gathering around her. Test the candle...

Belatedly she saw what Ben must be seeing, and realised that it suggested an intimacy she had never intended.

'It's a citronella candle,' she explained. 'It's supposed to deter midges. I wanted to know if it worked.'

'Of course.'

'Really.' She looked at him. Oh, no... 'I'm not...'

He cocked an eyebrow.

He didn't believe her. He thought she was trying to seduce him or something. As if she'd choose to do it with her useless cooking...

'I'm just not—okay!' she said, putting the glass down. Walking away. 'I'll go and get on with the next bit.'

Ben watched Ellie hurrying back to the kitchen. 'Pity...' he murmured. Pity.

The garden was absolutely still. For a while he stood there, considering exactly what that meant. Considering a future that suddenly seemed to have some meaning beyond work.

Needing a moment, he crossed the garden to the rabbit run, intending to shut Roger and Nigel away for the night. On an impulse he picked up the rabbit. He nervously burrowed his head down into the crook of his arm. Ben stroked him gently, reassuringly and after a moment he responded, looked up.

Ellie was right, he thought. He was warm. Gave back trust.

He tucked the pair of them up for the night, safe

from the urban fox he'd seen loping through the garden early in the morning.

He straightened, lingered, not quite ready to return to the kitchen and Ellie. The only sound was a black-bird filling the air with his liquid song, fighting off competition from the faint ringing of a telephone in a neighbouring garden.

Ellie was ruffling a fork through the couscous when he rejoined her in the kitchen, adding more water, not looking at him again.

'I suppose Natasha was a brilliant cook, too?' she said, tetchily.

'Cordon Bleu,' he assured her, casually helping himself to another pistachio as he crossed the kitchen. 'She could peel an onion without shedding a tear. She never got pink and flustered browning a piece of chicken,' he said, as she slapped at him with the fork. 'And if some small creature happened to drop on her while she was in the garden, she'd just pick it up like this…' ignoring the way she was glowering at him, he smiled, retrieved the small spider that was scaling her shoulder and heading for her neck '…and put it outside.'

He walked across to the door and dropped the inoffensive creature in the nearest flowerbed. When he returned, Ellie hadn't moved.

She tried to speak. Her mouth moved, but the words never made it.

He'd hoped that if he handled it calmly, without any drama, she'd see that it wasn't a big deal.

Apparently not.

Clearly she'd been underplaying it when she'd owned up to the screaming habdabs; she was beyond screaming, totally incoherent with fear.

'It's okay, Ellie,' he said. 'It's gone. You're all right.' For a moment she remained absolutely rigid. Then, with a shudder, she seemed to collapse against him and, putting his arms around her, he said it again. 'It's okay.'

Actually, with his arms around her it was. Very much okay. And in a gesture that was meant to comfort, reassure, he brushed his lips against her temple.

Then, because that had felt so good, he raised her hand to his lips, and she opened her eyes—not to react angrily, demand to know where he got off, but to look at him. Really look at him with those big brown eyes.

'Th-thank you,' she managed, then shivered again.

He drew her closer and she laid her head on his shoulder, and that was okay, too.

'Better?' he asked a few moments later, when she finally stopped shaking.

She looked up. 'Yes, thank you.' And her lips softened, parted in what might have been a smile, seemed much more. Need, invitation, he couldn't have said what. He didn't stop to analyse it, consider the consequences, but lowered his mouth to hers in something that wasn't so much a kiss, but a kind of recognition.

Ellie felt the shock of it to her toes. The way he'd gathered her in to keep her safe. The touch of his lips on her fingers, a gesture so unexpected, so tender, that it took her breath away.

She couldn't have said how it was she found herself pressed up close to him, her breasts crushed against his chest, her arms wound about his neck. Only that the brief brush of his firm lips against hers was like a jolt of energy, sending her pulse racing like a hundred-metre sprinter against the clock, even as it brought the world to a crashing halt around her. Made bells ring in her head...

Except that the bells weren't in her head. It was the chiming of the doorbell, and they both drew back, as if caught out.

She stepped back. 'The cavalry,' she said.

'I didn't send for them.'

No, but he was glad they'd arrived. She could see it in his face.

'No, I did.' She shrugged. 'I could see you didn't believe me about that candle.'

'You did ask me on a date.'

'I didn't!' Then, 'At least, I did. But not like that...' Damn, she was blushing again, she realised. 'No, honestly, Ben. I thought you might be more relaxed in a bigger party.'

'How much bigger?' he asked.

'Just Laura. Laura Morrison. Her house backs onto this one.'

'I know Laura.'

'Oh, right. Well, there's far too much food for just the two of us, anyway. She's on her own, and I owe her for the ferns.'

'I should have guessed that was where they came from.'

'She was really kind to me. And she helped me with the pansies, too.' On an impulse, she laid her folded hand against his cheek. 'You were kind, too. You handled the spider perfectly.'

'Any time. And by the way, Natasha wasn't a Cordon Bleu cook. I just said that to distract you.'

'Really?' She looked doubtful, shook her head, then turned as Laura tapped on the kitchen door, having walked in through the mud room.

'No one answered the door so I assumed you were in the garden.' She nodded at Ben. 'You've had a bit of excitement, I hear?'

'Nothing to get worked up about, Aunt Laura.'

Ellie looked at Ben, then at Laura. 'Aunt?'

'Ben's mother was my oldest sister. I stood for him at the font. Of course it took you to ask me to dinner, Ellie. If I'd waited for an invitation from Ben, I'd have starved.'

'Er, right,' she said, now totally embarrassed. 'Actually, since I'm cooking that still might happen. Come and tell me how you think the ferns are doing while Ben gets you a drink.'

As they went outside, Ben heard her say, 'How's the back?'

Ellie had summoned the cavalry—but for him, not for herself. She hadn't wanted to embarrass him, make him feel uncomfortable.

She hadn't had a clue that Laura was his aunt, or that relations had been somewhat strained between them following her undisguised delight that Natasha had chosen New York over him.

That Laura had responded to Ellie's invitation, prepared to risk sticking her head into the lion's den, suggested that she liked her a great deal. A rare accomplishment; his aunt was a very difficult woman to please—as Natasha had discovered to her cost. She wasn't used to being found wanting.

Ellie, he decided, taking a glass from the cupboard, pouring his aunt a drink and following them out into the garden, was a very unusual woman. Dizzy, irrational— it was totally irrational to fear small harmless creatures because they had too many legs—and lacking even the smallest degree of elegance. The kind of woman, in fact, that he couldn't imagine living with. And yet he was rapidly coming to the conclusion that living without her would be extremely dull.

He tracked them down to what had once been the kitchen garden by the simple expedient of following his aunt's carrying voice.

'Does he still keep in touch with the stick insect?' she was asking. He paused, hidden by the hedge. Ellie didn't answer, and his aunt pressed. 'Natasha?'

'I've no idea, Laura.'

'I do hope not. No woman should be that perfect. It's a crime against nature.' Ellie laughed, but not whole-heartedly, he thought. 'Any man who had the misfortune to love her would always be trailing in her wake.'

'He might be happy there.'

'For a while. But she'd soon get bored with that, don't you think? And, no matter how much he loved her, he'd be unhappy. A woman like that needs lovers, not a husband.'

'I think it's impossible for an outsider to understand what makes a marriage work.'

Laura laughed. 'I've rarely been put in my place so tactfully. But you're right. None of my business. Now, tell me about this herb garden you're thinking of planting.'

Ben joined them, handing Laura a highball glass containing straight single malt whisky, no water, no ice.

'Herb garden?' he asked. 'Is this going to involve another trip to the garden centre, Ellie?'

'Are you prepared to take the risk?' she asked, seizing this opportunity to change the subject. 'If you're holding fast about getting a dog, I might have to liberate a hamster...'

Laura's eyebrows rose, and Ellie embarked on a description of their last visit, including the rabbit rescue mission and Ben's heroic construction of the run, embellishing every little incident until his aunt was laughing so much that he had to rescue her drink.

Ellie grinned at him, then with a yelp exclaimed, 'The chicken!' and ran for the kitchen.

Laura glanced at him. 'That was fun.'

'Yes.'

'Come on,' she said, taking his arm. 'Let's go and see if she's managed to rescue dinner.'

Ellie had caught it just in time. At least she thought she had. She removed the chicken from the pan, added honey to the onions with a little more liquid. Tasted it.

'Does that taste burned to you?' she asked, offering Laura some of the sauce on a spoon.

'Add a drop of brandy. That fixes anything.'

'It *is* burned. I talk too much, that's my problem. My mother said I'd never make a cook until I learned to curb my tongue.'

'It's fine, really. Caramel is supposed to have that flavour.'

'Really?' She tried it again. The brandy Ben had sloshed in certainly gave it a kick.

An hour later they sat back, grinning. 'Not bad, Ellie,' Ben said. 'And next time you won't have as many distractions.'

'You're doing this again?' Laura asked. 'Can I come?'

'We were guinea pigs, Aunt Laura. Ellie is going to cook this for her sister's birthday.'

Laura glanced at her. 'You have a sister?'

'Stacey. Fortunately for my parents she's not like me. Being older, she got dibs on the common sense genes.'

'It's a common sense sort of name. Ellie is...livelier.

I imagine it's short for something? Ellen? Eleanor?'
There was something about the way Laura asked that
made her uneasy. But she wasn't the kind of woman
who'd buy *Milady*…

'Gabriella,' she said. With Ben sitting right there she
couldn't say anything else. Then, 'Did the citronella
candle work? Did anyone get bitten?'

'I never get bitten,' Ben said.

'Nor me. Hide like a rhinoceros.'

'Oh, well.'

'Another brandy, Aunt Laura?'

'No, thank you, dear. I couldn't manage another
thing. I'm ready for my bed.'

'I'll walk you home,' Ellie said.

'We both will.'

They saw her to the door. Laura kissed Ben, then
Ellie. 'Come and see me again soon, m'lady. We've a
lot to talk about.'

Ben took her arm in his. 'What was that about?'

'Um…' Her head was whirling. Clearly Laura knew
her secret. Why on earth hadn't she said something?
She looked back. Laura waved from the door, nodded
reassuringly.

Come soon.

Very soon…

'It's okay,' Ben was saying. 'I know she was having
a dig at Natasha earlier on.' He looked down her. 'And
I know you stopped her.'

Grabbing this unexpected lifeline, she said, 'Why
didn't you go with her, Ben? To New York.'

He stopped. Damn! She'd been so busy paddling
backwards that she hadn't seen the weir until she'd
fallen over it. Oh, well, in for a penny…

'She did want you to?'

He didn't deny it. 'It wouldn't have worked, Ellie. It wouldn't have been a partnership, two people working towards the same end. We might have occupied the same space, but we wouldn't have been together. Not in any way that mattered.'

'But if you loved her…'

'It wasn't easy, turning her down. Breaking the connection. Choosing to stay.' He glanced at her, his smile wry. 'She said I was a pathetic male who couldn't handle her success.'

'She didn't know you as well as you knew her.'

'Maybe. Maybe she had a point. I knew I'd have been a spectator in her life instead of living my own. Maybe a bigger man could have handled it. I realise it's a situation women have had to cope with since the year dot.'

'She wanted it all,' Ellie said.

'It's her right.'

'I'm not disputing that. But there's always a price to pay if you're a woman.'

'That's a very un-PC attitude, Ellie.'

'Is it? I thought I was just being realistic.'

'You don't believe there can ever be true equality?'

'When men start having babies.'

'Yes, well, there's that. If Tasha had stayed here, lived my fantasy, settling down as the academic wife, she'd have soon become restless, bored. She'd have felt trapped by motherhood…'

He let the words die and Ellie wondered if he, too, was thinking about his great-grandmother—the one who'd run off with her poet…

'I guess the truth is that neither of us was cut out to stand in someone else's wake, and that's the ultimate test, isn't it? Not whether you'd die for someone, the one-time ultimate sacrifice, but how much you'd be prepared to give up for them, day after day after day, for the rest of your life.'

'Is it?'

Ellie stood there for a moment, unable to think clearly. Or maybe, listening to the unravelling of Ben's relationship, she was thinking, seeing, more clearly than she ever had before. Because if that was the test, if she'd got it so right, why suddenly did it feel as if she'd got it wrong?

CHAPTER EIGHT

'THANKS, Ellie.'

'Um?'

Ben took her arm and they walked on in silence for a few moments, Ellie apparently lost in thought.

'For a great evening.'

Good conversation, laughter, the kind of evening he'd cut from his life, intimacy between friends a searing reminder of everything he'd lost. It was, he'd found, easier to be alone. Easier to bury himself in work.

Then, realising that she hadn't responded, 'Earth to Ellie?'

'What? Oh, sorry.' Then, 'Yes.'

Not exactly a ringing endorsement, although she'd seemed to be having a good time. 'You'll be able to cook for your sister without a worry in your head,' he said.

'What? Oh, yes.' Then, 'I had no idea that Laura was your aunt, Ben. Really. She knew I was living at Wickham Lodge, but she didn't say a word. If I'd known...'

'It's not a problem. I should have made my peace with her a long time ago. Better tonight than coming face to face at the wedding on Saturday, not knowing what to say.'

'Laura always knows what to say,' she said.

'And usually says it, whether you want to hear it or not. You will come? To the wedding?'

'If that's what you want,' she said, but he could see that, despite her effort to engage with him, she had slipped away again, was miles away in her head.

'Is it going to be that much of a burden?' he pushed, in an effort to draw her back. Wanting her quick smile, warm laughter.

'What?' She turned on him, as if to swat at an irritating wasp, then, focusing on him, she snapped back from whatever dark place she'd been. Found a smile. 'A burden? Oh, please.' Her laughter was warm, but he wasn't entirely convinced. 'Given the perfect excuse to buy a hat, who could possibly resist?'

'A hat? That I have to see.'

She gave him a sharp glance. Then, disappointingly, let it go. 'They only want what's best for you, you know. Family.'

'True, but while they may know what's best, they don't have to live with the consequences.' He glanced at her. 'Why did you really give up art, Ellie?'

'Who said I'd given it up?' she said, too quickly. 'I still draw. All the time.'

'When?'

'All the time. Just scribbles...' They'd rounded the side of the house, entered the courtyard. 'What a mess,' she said, pulling free as she saw the abandoned table, picking up a glass, holding it in front of her, using it as a way of distancing herself from him—afraid, perhaps, that, having kissed her once without being rebuffed, he'd assume he'd been given some kind of green light. That it was a short step from there to the bedroom.

Understandable, but she couldn't have been more wrong.

That he desired her, that his body would give him hell for not behaving like a caveman and going for instant satisfaction, was his problem, not hers.

He needed time to get used to the idea of actually wanting another woman. To deal with the surge of guilt that had followed that single kiss, the sense of betraying not Natasha, but himself. While Tasha had wasted no time in moving on in every way—much as it pained him to admit it, Laura had been right about the lovers— he'd believed in his love.

If it hadn't been as real, as strong, as he'd thought it, if his body could be roused, his head turned by the first woman who'd managed to get close to him since Tasha had left, how could he possibly trust his feelings?

More to the point, how could Ellie trust them?

He caught her wrist, held it, took the glass from her hand. 'Leave it, Ellie, I'll clear up.'

He was close enough to feel the warmth of her skin, smell the familiar herby scent of the shampoo that she used. Beneath his hand, her wrist felt fine, delicate, and it took an effort of will to release her, to deny himself even the innocent pleasure of kissing her cheek. There would, he knew, be nothing innocent about it. Instead he took a step back, leaving the way clear to the door.

'I'll see you tomorrow, Ellie. If you're not too busy maybe we could take that trip to the garden centre. If you're really thinking about replanting the old herb garden.'

'I hadn't got beyond the thought,' she said. 'Besides...' He didn't help her out. 'It's not my garden. I can't just start doing stuff.'

'That's never stopped you before.'

'Curtains, ferns…' she said.

And a lot more. But she looked so utterly miserable that he couldn't keep up the teasing.

'It's okay, Ellie. If I didn't want you changing things I'd say so. What would it take? To restore the herb garden?'

She shrugged. 'It would need planning. A planting design…'

'That's your department. Why don't you sketch something out?'

'I don't know anything about gardening.'

'Like cooking? Between us we managed.'

Ellie knew she wouldn't sleep. Didn't want to think. Did not, despite her proclaimed enthusiasm for it, want to confront reality. And she would find no release staring at a blank screen, battling with words that wouldn't come. Since she'd started writing her column, her attempts to write anything else had been a complete waste of time.

Instead, she took out the sketchpad she'd bought for her *Milady* drawings, a fine pen, curled up on the sofa. She'd found the bones of the original herb garden, the overgrown brick paths, when she'd been hunting for green stuff for the animals, and it had occurred to her that the renovation of a herb garden could be used as an on-running theme in her column.

She'd intended to pick Laura's brains for ideas for a planting scheme; that was now out of the question. Clearly since the last time they'd met she'd seen the *Milady* issue with the 'ferns' column, put two and two together, and she'd know exactly what Ellie was up to. At least that had been all her own work—even if it had

only been in her head until Laura had given her the
ferns to match her imagination.

This time it seemed she was going to have to do all
the work herself. The planning, at least. As for the rest
of it, well, the idea of working side by side with Ben—
as she had this evening, preparing supper—made the
whole thing feel much more real. Much more appealing.

For a while she worked on a plan, checking out the
plants Laura had suggested against a book she'd
borrowed from the library. After a while she found the
lack of colour irritating, and hunted through a small tin
trunk in which she kept the kind of stuff that she
couldn't bear to throw away, found the box of precious
oil pastels that her mother had given her years before.

Two rows of barely used colours. She ran her fingers
over them, breathing in the scent of them, the feel of the
new sticks under her fingers. Choosing the colours.
Blending them to make the glaucous grey-green of
lavender, rosemary, using hot orange and yellow and
white for the glowing brightness of pot marigolds, pale
pink for the flowers on low spreading thyme...

When it was done she ripped the sheet from the pad,
carried on.

She drew the kitchen table covered with small dishes,
each containing a spice or some other ingredient of the
dish she'd cooked with Ben.

She drew the heavy red cast-iron pot, shining with
heat and colour on the top of the Aga.

She drew the table set for two. Pristine, fresh, with
its blue cloth, pale candle.

Drew it again with crumpled napkins, crumbs, the
candle burned low, Ben's hand around a glass, his strong
wrist; the rest of him was out of the picture, but she

could see him clearly, leaning back in the chair, laughing at some memory he'd shared with Laura.

She drew and drew and drew, ripping pages from her pad as she filled them, dropping them on the floor.

Images stored in her memory poured out on the paper. She drew the garden from her window. The porch trailed with honeysuckle, her bike propped up against it.

The soft, warm rose and peach colours of the bricks of Wickham Lodge. The mock medieval turret. The wisteria, its thick twisted grey stems, long blue racemes echoed in the slate of the roof.

She drew a detail of the newel post, furniture she polished and knew as intimately as her own hand, the fold of the shawl over the sofa. She drew swift sketches of the people she worked for, producing in a few lines a feature, a look, going back further and further until her slashing pastels produced Sean, lying in the road, the small hi-tech headphones still blaring out the blast of noise that had masked the sound of the approaching car. His hand resting against the bloodied headline proclaiming United's triumph in the league.

'How dare you?' she demanded. Slash, slash, slash. Her tears puddled in the red, so that it ran into the black just as it had on that hideous day. 'How dare you be so careless? So thoughtless? How dare you die?'

She caught her breath on a sob, and in the sudden awful silence she heard the sound of a bird, whistling up the dawn. Shocked, she looked up, saw the pale arch of early pre-dawn grey against light. Heard a step, turned, and saw Ben standing in the open doorway, hair tousled from bed, wearing only a pair of cut-off jogging pants, his bare feet pushed into old tennis pumps.

'There was a vixen in the garden,' he said, as if that

explained everything. 'She can't get at Roger, but she's like you, Ellie, just won't quit. So I went out to chase her off. That's when I saw your light. You've been up all night.'

Not a question.

She was still wearing the same clothes, jeans, a T-shirt; it wouldn't take a genius to see that she hadn't been to bed.

She let the pad fall to her knee, rubbed a hand across her face, eased her shoulders. 'What time is it?'

'Just after five.'

She nodded. 'About time I was up, anyway,' she said, attempting to make light of it.

'Why don't you give it a miss today, Ellie?'

She blinked. She looked that bad, huh? 'I can't,' she said. 'People are relying on me.'

'They will manage for once.' He came close, knelt in front of her, said, 'It's your turn to call in favours.'

She tried to look somewhere else, ignore the wide smooth gold of shoulders that lived up to the promise offered by his tweed jacket, the highlights and shadows of silky skin that made her fingers twitch—not for her pastels to reproduce them, but to reach out and touch. The faint shadow of hair that arrowed to a point as it dived below the sagging waist of his pants. Only the puckered cicatrice of a scar across his shoulder, down one arm, marred his beauty. Recent. Only just beginning to fade.

'If only it were that easy,' she said, resisting the urge to run a finger along it, take the pain to herself. 'I have to pick up Daisy Thomas from nursery school at twelve. No one else can do that. It has to be someone they know.'

'Give me Sue's number. I'll call her and tell her you'll pick up Daisy, but you'll have to pass on everything else today.'

'No…'

'I'm not giving you a choice, Ellie. Go to bed, get some sleep. I'll wake you in plenty of time.'

She knew he was right. She didn't feel fit to lift a duster, let alone wield a vacuum cleaner, and she needed to be alert to keep up with three-year-old Daisy. 'Promise? If I don't turn up—'

'You have my word, Ellie. I won't let you down.'

No. He had the straightest look of any man she'd ever known. He was honest, forthright. Everything she was not.

'Her number's on the Busy Bees card. It's pinned to the board.'

'I'll get it when I've seen you safely down to your room.'

'I can manage…' She tried to move. Her legs were locked beneath her, her hands stiff. Ben took the pad from her, doing his best not to look at the shocking image, but it was compelling in its awfulness. And he must have heard her… 'I was so angry with him,' she said. 'Not just about the milk.'

Without warning, Ben found himself recalling an occasion when he'd been angry with Natasha when, without consulting him, she'd arranged an evening out with some visiting politicians from eastern Europe, booking a table at some exotic restaurant. Stimulating for her, hard work for him, when all he'd wanted after a day of financial hassle and university politics was something on a tray in front of the fire. On the surface the row had been about one evening, quickly forgotten. In retrospect it had been a metaphor for their whole relationship.

'It's never just about the milk, Ellie,' he said. 'You gave up art college for him, didn't you?'

'I gave it up for me. We were Ellie-and-Sean. Sean-and-Ellie. That's all I ever wanted. The two of us. Kids. He had no right to be so careless with his life.'

Not when she'd sacrificed her dreams for a lifetime of happy-ever-after with him.

How dare you...?

He looked at the angry strokes of colour, impression rather than reality, but a powerful image nonetheless. Unlike the prettier pictures that littered the floor, this one was filled with rage, pain and loss.

'Did you ever take the balloon ride, Ellie? Not the metaphorical one, but the real thing?'

He didn't think she was going to answer him, but after a moment she nodded. Then, as if to make sure he understood, 'I took Sean's ashes and set him free over the Downs, poured two glasses of champagne. One for him, one for me. Too late. We left everything too late.'

'Let it go, Ellie,' he said, a twist on her lips telling him to move on. But, whatever she was doing, he was certain now that it was anything but that. 'You have to let it go.'

He laid the pad to one side, took the pastel from her numb fingers, then stood up, easing her to her feet before she fell asleep where she was. Held her when her legs refused to support her.

'They've gone to sleep,' she said.

'Very sensible. Let's get you downstairs so that you can join them.'

He hooked his arm around her waist, helped her to the next floor, tugged back the cover, sat her on the bed. She fell back against the pillows. 'Jeans, Ellie,' he said. Then, clearly to himself, 'You can't sleep in your jeans.'

He unbuttoned the waistband, eased them down over

her hips, over her feet, lifted her legs onto the bed, then covered her up, kissed her cheek. She turned over, face into the pillow, as if to shut out the light—or the world.

He would have drawn the curtains, but she'd taken down the heavy velvets, draped soft sheers in their place. Covered the bed with a hand-pieced quilt in shades of blue. Made the room entirely hers.

Beside the bed was a silver frame.

Sean. Smiling.

He had every reason…

He watched Ellie for a moment, but she didn't stir and he finally went back upstairs to fetch Sue's number. It was too early to call, so he gathered up the drawings, looking at each one as he shuffled them into a tidy pile, smiling at the layout of the herb garden, the neat detailing of the plants, Latin and common names. The drawing of Wickham Lodge.

Coming to a halt at the one of the table at the end of their meal, his hand resting on the cloth, his fingers curled around a glass. Hands, he knew, were notoriously difficult to bring off successfully, but this, drawn from memory, was superb. He rubbed at his knuckles, at the almost forgotten scar that she'd caught.

She was, it seemed, truly gifted. Even if she'd wanted to stay near Sean, if he'd had no choice but to stay in the area, there was an excellent art department at the university where she could have studied.

What had she said? Exactly? Something about the common sense option. He looked again at the drawing and wondered who had persuaded her that taking an English degree with its limited options was the common sense choice.

He realized, to his chagrin, that he'd underestimated

her. If she'd had that wide a choice, she must have been a seriously bright student.

Maybe she could write as well as she could draw.

He glanced around, half hoping to find something, anything that would give him a clue. But there was nothing lying around that he could pick up. And he wouldn't stoop to looking through her drawers.

Instead, he picked up her design for the herb garden and, after a moment's hesitation, the picture of the house, leaving the rest in a neat pile on the table beside the sofa, took the Busy Bees card and went downstairs. There was a handwritten cellphone number beside the printed office number, and on impulse he dialled that.

'Sue Spencer.' The voice was crisp, collected, wide awake despite the early hour. Clearly Sue Spencer worked as hard as the people she employed.

'Miss Spencer, this is Ben Faulkner at Wickham Lodge. I'm calling to let you know that Ellie won't be at work today.'

'Is she sick?' He heard genuine concern, rather than the vexed reaction of a disgruntled employer who'd have to find a replacement at short notice.

'Not sick. She just didn't get much sleep.' Then, because that could be taken more than one way, 'She was working.'

'Writing.' A heartfelt sigh. Adele, it seemed, was not the only person who was concerned that Ellie was wasting her life. At least he could reassure her on that score.

'Not writing. She was drawing.'

'Drawing?' There was a pause. 'Drawing what?'

'Anything and everything. She produced dozens of sketches—things, furniture, people. A quite detailed picture of the house.'

'Oh, well, she fell in love with your house the first time she saw it.'

'Did she?'

Somehow, he was not surprised. That was the difference between the way it had looked when Mrs Turner worked for him and now. The fact that his mother's precious ornaments were no longer placed in regimented rows, but in small groups. That there were flowers. That it looked like home.

It was love.

'I found her in a bit of a state at about five o'clock this morning.'

'Oh, Lord.' Then, 'How is she?'

'Exhausted. Asleep. She made me promise to wake her in time to pick up Daisy Thomas.'

'Right. Yes, that would have been difficult. Tell her I'll sort out cover for the rest of her jobs. Tell her... Tell her to take the rest of the week off, will you?'

'I'll tell her. I can't promise she'll listen.'

'Maybe if you tell her that I won't pay her even if she does turn up, that would do it.'

'But would she believe you?'

She laughed. 'You've got her measure, Ben.'

'I wouldn't go that far. Why don't you drop by this evening and tell her in person? She might need someone to talk to. Someone she trusts.'

'I'm not sure that's me any more. She's cut herself off in the last few months. Stopped talking about anything, even her writing.' Then, when he didn't respond, 'Maybe I should have tried harder. You're right. I'll be there. And Ben...?'

'Yes?'

'Thank you for taking care of her.'

'No problem.' Then, 'Miss Spencer…?'

'Sue, please.'

'Sue. Would you say it's a good thing? That Ellie's drawing again?'

'It's certainly a breakthrough.' Then, 'How much has she told you?'

'About her dead husband who wanted to take the balloon ride. That she's given up teaching to write a novel. That studying art was not the common sense option.'

'That much?'

Her evident surprise made him feel privileged, included. 'Was he jealous?' he asked. 'Of her talent?'

'Sean? He adored her, Ben.'

'I never doubted it.' He'd seen the man's smile. The eyes suggested he had everything he wanted. 'It doesn't answer my question, though.'

'She adored him.'

He'd never doubted that, either, but to hear it from someone who'd known Ellie all her life, known Sean, was both a comfort and a pain.

'Maybe that does,' he said.

'Ellie?'

Surfacing from the dark pit of sleep, Ellie took a moment to work out where she was. Her head hurt, her gritty eyes refused to open, just as they had morning after morning for months when every night she'd cried herself to sleep. When every morning she'd dragged herself out of bed, plastered a smile on her face and stood in front of her class, going through the motions of another day.

'You asked me to wake you. To fetch Daisy.'

Ben!

She sat up, suddenly wide awake, remembering, groped for her alarm clock, blinking at it, trying to focus, work out which was the big hand, which the little one.

'You've got plenty of time.'

'Sue? Did you call Sue?' She dragged her fingers through hair that was sticking up in a tangled bush, saw the state of her hands, covered with pastel colour. Swung her legs over the side of the bed, then realised that she was wearing nothing but a T-shirt and a pair of pants. Decided not to worry about it.

Ben had seen her legs before, when she was tidy. He'd managed to contain himself then, so it was unlikely he'd lose it when she looked a total mess.

'Slow down,' he said. 'I've spoken to Sue. She said you were to take the rest of the week to recover.'

'Recover? What on earth did you tell her?'

'You can ask her yourself. She'd coming to see you this evening.'

'Oh.' She'd been avoiding Sue. She could read her too well, would know she was hiding something. 'Now I'm really worried.'

'Don't be. I've brought you a cup of tea and some toast—'

'I don't have time for that,' she said. 'I've got to go. You should have called me sooner. It'll take me twenty minutes to walk—'

'But only five minutes in the car.'

She shook her head. 'I don't need…' She swallowed. 'If you'd just called me.'

'I did. You've got half an hour. Take your time.'

He didn't give her a chance to argue, but without him the room suddenly felt horribly empty. She picked up a piece of thick, buttery toast, bit into it as she walked into the bathroom, instantly lost her appetite as she caught sight of herself in the mirror.

The hair was bad, but she'd expected that. Her fingers, nails, were ingrained with colour. Not good to go to bed that way, but the sheets would wash. It was the streaks and smudges of pastel, red and green and black, across her forehead, on her cheeks, down her neck, that made her flinch. She dropped the toast into the bin, spread out her hands. Her fingers hurt, her hands ached. She remembered the wild night, how the images had poured from her. Ben prising the pastels from her fingers, helping her downstairs. After that everything was a blank.

She looked down at her legs. Just as well she hadn't thrown a wobbly over bare legs, since he must have helped her out of her jeans before he tucked her up in bed.

She tried not to think about that and, wasting no time, stripped off the rest of her clothes and dived under the shower. It took her less than five minutes to wash her hair, scrub herself clean of the war paint.

She towelled her hair dry, dressed swiftly, and in ten minutes was downstairs, with nothing on her face but a film of moisturiser, wearing a short-sleeved shirt and a neat skirt that had been part of her schoolmarm wardrobe, her damp hair screwed back in a French plait.

Ben got to his feet as she walked through the kitchen, beat her to the door.

'Don't disturb yourself. I'm not an invalid.' He was blocking the door. 'Really, Ben, I'm quite capable of walking to the nursery school.'

'I never suggested you weren't, but I thought we might all go straight to the garden centre, have lunch there. We could take Daisy to visit the pets and then buy some plants.' He held up the plan she'd drawn. 'Since you've done all the hard work.' Then, 'Of course, if you think the little girl would be happier at home—'

Ellie swallowed. She'd hoped that if she just waltzed through the kitchen with a wave he'd see that she was back to normal, let her go. Be glad to forget the fact that he'd kissed her. Wipe last night from his mind.

If only she could. Put the clock back. All she could do was put things right. But not now. This needed more than ten minutes.

'Yes?' he said, prompting her for an answer.

She shook her head. 'I'd planned to make sandwiches, take her for a walk along the river, feed the ducks, buy her an ice cream.'

'There's no time to make sandwiches. And the ducks won't starve.' She looked at him. Fatal… 'The garden centre has ice cream,' he added temptingly.

'Are you sure?'

'Positive. I noticed the freezer last time we were there.'

'I meant about spending the afternoon…' She waited for him to take the chance to back down. When he didn't she gave an awkward little shrug. 'I know how busy you are.'

Busy? Ben considered the word in the context of the work he was doing. 'The text I'm working on has been waiting for me for over five thousand years. I don't imagine one more afternoon will make much difference in the great scheme of things,' he said.

'If you put it like that.'

'I do.' And, as if the matter were settled, he stood back to let her by before opening the car door for her, waiting until she was installed in the front seat of Adele's ancient Morris, with her seat belt safely fastened, before he added, 'Of course I will want something in return.'

She froze. 'Oh?'

'Relax, Ellie, your virtue is safe. If it was your body I was after, trust me, I'd want your wholehearted co-operation.' Then, grinning, 'The way your cheeks get involved when you blush.'

He didn't wait for her hot denial, but closed the door and slid in beside her, deciding that if he was going to do much of this he was going to have to buy another car.

'You drew a picture of the house,' he said, as he fitted the key into the ignition. This time his words had the totally opposite effect. 'You've seen it?' she said, the colour draining from her face.

Damn! She thought he'd invaded her privacy, and she was right, he had...

'I know I shouldn't have looked through your pictures,' he said quickly, in an attempt to forestall the anticipated eruption. 'I just meant to pick them up, but they were so striking. They have a real leap-off-the-paper quality.' She didn't respond. Maybe, like him, she wasn't able to get that last terrible image out of her mind. 'I've always thought the house looked at its best with the wisteria in full bloom,' he said, hoping to distract her.

'Wisteria? Oh, right.' She seemed to sag a little. 'Last night. I drew it last night.'

What had she thought he meant? Had she drawn it before?

'It's no more than a scribble, Ben. You can't possibly want it.'

'I'm sure Picasso said that when he drew sketches on paper napkins.'

'I'm quite sure he didn't. He knew his worth. But in any case, I'm no Picasso.'

'So I can have the picture?'

'That's all you wanted?'

That wasn't what he'd meant, but she seemed so jumpy he didn't tease. 'That's all.' For now.

She shrugged. 'Take it. It's yours.'

'Thank you.'

Normally she would have looked at him, smiled. Instead she looked at her wristwatch, despite the fact that there was a clock on the dashboard right in front of her, and said, 'It's time we were leaving, Ben.'

CHAPTER NINE

ELLIE expected Daisy to be shy with Ben, but he was the one who lifted her up so that she could choose her lunch. It was his hand she clung to as they looked at the rabbits. He was the one who carried her as they toured the nursery, rubbing leaves so that she could smell the different herbs. Laughing as she screwed up her face and shuddered at something she didn't like.

'It's no good buying them individually, like this,' Ellie said, taking a pot of lemon balm from Ben. 'If you're serious about reviving the garden as it was originally laid out, you're going to need dozens of plants.' He didn't answer and she looked up. Daisy was curled trustingly in the crook of his arm, her head on his shoulder, and without warning she felt the prickle of tears. 'They don't even have everything on the list,' she said crossly. 'This is a waste of time.'

'Maybe we should get in a professional?'

We? There was such temptation in the word, such promise. Such pain.

'No!' It wasn't the suggestion of professional help that she was refusing. He regarded her thoughtfully, those clear blue eyes seeing far too much. She shook her head. 'I didn't mean…' She'd never meant it to go this far. To get this complicated. 'You don't have to.'

'The garden, like the house, has been neglected for years. It was my mother's passion.'

'Oh? Like Laura, then.' She was gripping the plastic pot so tightly that it was in danger of cracking, and she carefully replaced it back in the display. 'Her garden is lovely.'

'My mother designed it, laid it out with my grand-mother. Laura was still at school then.'

She frowned. 'Your mother lived there, too?' Then, catching on, 'She was the girl next door?'

'She and my father grew up together. Like you and Sean.'

She didn't want to talk about Sean. Had been doing her best not to think about him. If she let him into her thoughts he'd know she'd kissed Ben. Had wanted him to kiss her. 'He never considered marrying again?' she asked. 'Your father?'

'It wasn't something he ever discussed with me, Ellie. He was a very private man.' Then, 'I suspect Laura hoped he might, given time, notice her. She never married.'

'Oh. Poor Laura.'

'Life isn't that…tidy. The truth is, he was never inter-ested in anything very much after my mother died. He hung on until he thought I was old enough to manage without him, then he just let go.'

An aging father, a teenage girl, a small boy. 'It must have been hard for him. For all of you.'

'We coped. Nannies. Housekeepers. And Laura was always there.' He looked down at Daisy. 'Are you ready for that ice cream, miss?' She giggled, wriggled, and he set her down. 'Go and pick out the one you want.'

'Not a good idea. She'll choose some brightly coloured lolly that'll have her whizzing about like a demon.'

'Isn't that what kids are meant to do?'

'Not if they're being fuelled by chemical colourings.'

'Spoilsport. What time do we have to get her back to her mother?'

'She's usually home by four. She goes to the hospital twice a week for dialysis. On Tuesday and Friday.'

'It's kidney failure?' He looked at Daisy and, without being told, Ellie knew that was what had taken his mother from him.

'She's waiting for a transplant, Ben.'

'My father gave my mother one of his kidneys. Her body rejected it. He never talked about it. Adele told me.'

For once she didn't know what to say. Finally managed, 'Things are better now.'

'Yes.' Then he turned to her, 'Four o'clock? Plenty of time to fit in the ducks.'

He bought them all ice lollies layered in traffic light colours of red, green and yellow. When Ellie gave him a look that suggested he'd regret it, he grinned and said, 'I always wanted to try one of these.'

'You are such a liar, Ben Faulkner. And, to prove it, your tongue will turn purple.'

'That's life with you around, Ellie March. Every day a new experience.'

Sue arrived at eight, bearing a pizza of stupendous proportions.

'We can't eat all this—'

'I have only one thing to say to that,' she replied, putting the box on the table, along with a bottle of wine. 'Extra anchovies.'

'But we'll do our best.'

Sue grinned. 'Corkscrew?' Then, as she tackled the bottle while Ellie found some glasses, sorted out plates, 'Actually, I bought the biggest because I thought Ben would be here.'

Actually, she'd thought he would be, too. Had planned to sit him down as soon as they'd dropped Daisy off at home, make a clean breast of things. Own up to the *Milady* column. Tell him that her drawing of his house was appearing on a monthly basis in the magazine.

Instead, he'd dropped her off at the gate, said he had some things to do. She suspected he just wanted to put a little distance between them after the closeness of the past twenty-four hours. Starting with that kiss…

Her lips softened, warmed at the memory, and, realising that Sue was watching her, she snapped back to now. 'You two must have had a very cosy chat this morning,' she said briskly.

'Only about you. Were your ears burning?'

'My ears, like the rest of me, were asleep.' Then, because the idea of Sue and Ben talking about her was slightly disturbing, 'Should I be worried?'

'No. I was the soul of discretion.'

'There's nothing in my life to be indiscreet about.'

'I know. You're a real disappointment to me. But I have high hopes of Ben. The man is a dish. Bright, too. Books, papers—you name it, he's written it.'

'Checked him out on the university website, did you?'

'I just have your best interests at heart.'

'You were just being nosy.' Then, because talking about Ben was a lot easier than facing a grilling from Sue about last night, 'Well, don't keep me in suspense. I know there's more.'

'Well, obviously.' Sue finally pulled the cork, filled two glasses. 'The university website was fine as far as it went, but—and I did this purely in the spirit of sisterly friendship—I Googled him.'

'You are so bad.'

Sue regarded her thoughtfully. 'Are you telling me you were never tempted?'

'I'm telling you I resisted.'

'Really? That's…telling. What were you afraid you'd find?'

Ellie refused to bite. The truth was it had never occurred to her to go snooping on the net. She knew Benedict Faulkner was a distinguished academic. His sister had told her that when she'd first started working at Wickham Lodge. She was also aware that he'd written books on his forensic examination of ancient languages. They were on his shelves. If she'd ever bothered to do the decent thing, take one out and dust it, she have seen his photograph on the cover.

'Did you know that he led a party of refugees over the mountains to escape the fighting in Kirbeckistan?'

What? 'He told me that a group of them had walked out.'

'Walked? Have you seen what it's like there? A woman who was in the party talked to one of the redtops. Obviously completely smitten, but there's no doubt that the man is a hero.'

'Oh, please. If you're prepared to believe anything printed in a tabloid newspaper.' Except, of course, she could believe it. Just as she could believe that some woman had fallen for him. What about him? Not love. He was still in love with Natasha Perfect. But in life-threat-ening situations people clung to each other. And he'd stayed with someone, he'd said. When he'd got home. Someone who'd taken care of him. Tended that wound.

She felt a surge of jealousy so overpowering that for a moment she couldn't think. Couldn't hear. Just clenched her fists, closed her eyes.

'Ellie?'

She started. Realised that Sue was looking at her a little oddly.

'Are you okay?'

'Fine. Still a bit tired. Sorry, what were you saying?'

'Nothing. Just wondering why you're still here, that's all. As a house-sitter you must be redundant.'

'Ben will be going away again soon. It made sense for me to stay.' She pushed back a trailing wisp of hair. 'It's a huge house. We hardly ever see one another.'

'You get close enough to talk. And don't think of denying it.'

'I wasn't going to,' she protested, wondering what on earth Ben had said, stuffing pizza into her mouth to give herself thinking time. 'You know me,' she said, when she'd managed to swallow it, then taken a sip of wine. 'I never did know when to shut up, and he always seems to catch me with my guard down.'

'Well, that's promising. How far down?'

Further down than she'd ever imagined. He'd kissed her... Then, realising that Sue was regarding her through suspiciously narrowed eyes, she snatched her hand away from her mouth.

'I hurt my knee,' she said. 'He gave me a lift, that's all.' Then, because the one way to distract Sue was to make her laugh, she shrugged and said, 'Well, apart from the compost.'

'The compost?' she repeated.

'And the rabbit. And the herb garden.'

'Rabbit!'

She pretended to bang the side of her head. 'There seems to be an echo in here.'

'Very funny. Okay. Back up. Start at the beginning.' Success...

'Where to? The lift? It was nothing.' Almost nothing. 'Ben startled me, I fell off a ladder, fortunately I landed on him.' She described the scene, the interesting exchange of views.

By the time she got to the part where Ben's spectacles had fallen to bits in her hand, Sue was practically crying with laughter.

'I don't believe a word of it,' she declared.

'It's true! Every word.' Well, nearly every word. But why spoil a good story by sticking to the truth? 'Anyway, having maimed me, he had no choice but to strap me up and drive me to the Chamber of Commerce reception.'

'And then you talked?'

'You know how it is,' she said. 'You sit there with your trousers round your ankles while someone straps an ice bandage around your knee. You have to say something, and "ouch" gets a bit monotonous.' Uh-oh. That was the trouble with storytelling. Knowing when to stop... 'He didn't think I should go,' she said. 'To the Chamber of Commerce.'

'He was right.' Sue clearly wanted to ask about the trousers-round-the-ankles scenario, but surprisingly let it go. 'Tell me about the rabbit,' she said.

'Roger? Oh, well, I needed some compost for the ferns...' Sue looked as if she was about to interrupt, decided against it '...and Ben took me to the garden centre because obviously I couldn't fetch it on my bike.'

'Obviously.'

'And while I was there I went to look at the rabbits. Do you remember them, Sue?'

'I remember you wanting one and your mum having none of it.'

'Mmm. Well, there was this little black one.'

'And you bought it?'

'Roger. And Nigel. He's a guinea pig. Ben built them a run.'

'That's quite a conversation you've had. He seems a very indulgent…' She paused. 'Not landlord. What is he, exactly?'

'House-mate?' Ellie offered. 'And, yes, I suppose he is. He even ate my cooking.'

'You *cooked* for him?'

'No!' She laughed. Ha, ha, ha… 'Not *for* him.'

Sue's surprise was understandable. She had never even cooked for Sean. But then he'd been so much better at it than she was.

'I just needed someone to taste what I'd cooked.' And somehow, despite her determination not to tell, the entire story just spilled out. *Milady.* The column. Lady Gabriella…

'Wait! *Wait!*' Sue said, her eyes widening with horrified fascination—and entirely missing the impressive point that Ellie was now a columnist for a national magazine. 'You not only somehow convinced this Cochrane woman that you're "Lady Gabriella March…"' she punctuated the air with quote marks '…but that you have three children? How old are they?'

'Well, Oliver is eight. He's really musical. Sings in the choir. Sasha is six and pony mad. Chloe is just a toddler.' In the face of Sue's open-mouthed disbelief, she said, 'Stacey loaned me one of her suits. I looked older.'

'Even so, you'd have had to have been married at eighteen with a honeymoon baby.' Then, perhaps remembering that that had been her dream, Sue said, 'So, does the heroic Ben know he's playing the role of the fictitious Sir Benedict Faulkner?'

'No! I mean he's not.' Sue didn't look convinced. 'Honestly. This started before Ben came home.' Then she'd written about him building the rabbit pen... 'Besides,' she said, 'my title is a courtesy one.'

'What does that mean?'

'That it's mine, nothing to do with the fictitious husband.' Sue still looked blank. 'That my father is an earl or something?' she offered.

'You are in so much trouble, Ellie March,' Sue said, grinning as she cut them both another slice of pizza, sucked the juices off her thumb. 'No wonder you're having trouble sleeping.'

'It was just one night.' Then, 'What did Ben say? This morning.'

'Just that you'd had a sleepless night.' She smiled. 'He was such a gentleman. When he realised he might have given entirely the wrong impression, he went to great pains to make sure I didn't think that it was the result of a night on the tiles.'

'As if.'

'Well, indeed. The thought never crossed my mind which, when you think about it, is pretty sad. We haven't got a life between us. Not a real one, anyway.' She chewed meditatively on her pizza for a moment, then said, 'He did ask me about Sean.'

'Oh?' Ellie couldn't quite place the feeling that

clenched at her stomach. A frisson of satisfaction that he was interested enough to want to know about the man she'd loved? Or was it nothing more than irritation that he should go behind her back and pry? Or both? 'What, exactly, did he want to know?'

'If Sean was jealous of your talent.'

'What?' All afternoon she'd been racked with guilt. Now she discovered that he'd been maligning Sean. 'That's outrageous!'

'Uh-oh. Big mouth, large foot...' Sue picked up the bottle, topped up both of their glasses. 'If it's any help, sweetie, I'm sure he was just concerned about you. He'd seen your drawings,' she pointed out, as if that was enough. 'Let's face it, none of us understood why you chose English over Art.'

'It wasn't complicated. I just wanted an ordinary life, Sue. I wanted to be married to Sean. To have children.'

'You could have taught art.'

'No,' she said. 'I couldn't.'

And because she didn't want to think about it any more, and because she knew it would divert Sue as nothing else could, she said, 'Ben has invited me to go with him to a family wedding on Saturday.'

'Oh?'

'Only because he doesn't want people to think he's a sad bastard who hasn't got a girl. Or a closet gay.'

'He's not, is he?'

'No!' Then, when Sue smiled, wished she hadn't been quite so emphatic. 'He's definitely not a bastard. His parents were childhood sweethearts.'

'It's not as rare as you'd think, then? So, who are you going as? Ellie March or Lady Gabriella?'

'Myself,' she replied.

'You'll be wearing a pair of extra fine Marigolds and a Busy Bees sweatshirt, then?'

Ellie stowed a new pair of the bright yellow rubber gloves she wore to protect her hands in her backpack. It would serve Ben right if she did appear on Saturday morning wearing them, and her Busy Bees sweatshirt.

Sean. Jealous.

Obviously that was what everyone thought, she realised as she fetched her bike from the shed. Sue hadn't said as much, but it had been there, in her voice. In everything she *hadn't* said.

She'd just mounted her bike when a pick-up truck reversed through the gates and began backing up towards the kitchen garden, forcing her to swerve.

'Hey!' she said. 'Where do you think you're going?'

The driver stopped alongside her, grinned. 'We're doing some clearance work for Ben.' Then, 'You must be Ellie. Any chance of a cup of tea before we start?'

'I couldn't say. Why don't you wake Ben and ask him?'

She didn't wait for a reply, didn't even know if Ben was home. She didn't stop to find out. He'd organised the clearance squad, he could give them tea and biscuits. She rode on, ignoring the whistle of appreciation that followed her.

'Moron,' she muttered.

Clearance work?

Was that where he'd gone yesterday after he'd dropped her? To organise some heavy labour? He really meant to go ahead with the herb garden?

All through an unusually long day, catching up with some of the people she'd missed the day before, after

Ellie had convinced Sue she was fit enough to work, her head wouldn't let it go.

She'd already decided not to continue the column after the six-month initial contract. She already felt bad enough about it. But telling Sue had somehow made it all much more real. Much more dangerous. Much less a triumph.

She still had three to write, however, and she'd already mentioned the overgrown herb garden. Restoring it would offer something less personal to write about, and finishing with the completed garden would round things off. Make a suitable ending.

By the time she got home, just after four, the pick-up had gone, and she went straight to the kitchen garden to see what they'd done. Ben was there, tending to the dying remains of a bonfire at one end of the plot. At the far end, hundreds of young plants in trays had been laid out, waiting to be planted.

'When you make your mind up to do something, Doc,' she said, feeling oddly defensive, 'you don't hang about, do you?'

'Laura found me someone who could clear the ground quickly. And a nursery for the herbs.'

'That's where you were yesterday evening?'

She half expected him to ask her about the *Milady* column. Instead he grinned, said, 'You missed me?'

Laura hadn't told…

'Sue missed you. She wanted to see if you lived up to your internet billing.' Then, before he could comment, 'You're going to be busy.'

'This was your idea, Ellie. I'm relying on you to pitch in and help.'

'Me? I know nothing about gardening.'

'Neither do I, but how hard can it be? You make a hole, drop in a plant.'

'There's got to be more to it than that.'

'I suspect you're right, but it's a beginning. There's something in the potting shed that might help.'

'Alan Titchmarsh? Gift-wrapped?' she asked hopefully. 'Cuddly, good-looking, the country's favourite television gardener?' He didn't answer. 'Not the entire *Ground Force* team? Tell me it's the *Ground Force* garden makeover team?'

'Gift-wrapped is all I can offer. As for the rest, it's just you and me,' he said, sticking the fork he was holding into the ground.

The box lying on the bench in the potting shed was indeed gift-wrapped. It wasn't very big, but the red bow more than made up for that. She tugged on the ribbon, lifted the lid to reveal the stainless steel trowel she'd been looking at on their first visit to the garden centre. She picked it up, felt the weight of it, the smoothness of the polished wooden handle. It was a fine tool.

The perfect gift.

The promise of partnership, of working together, being together. The promise of her future here, in his house.

She turned, knowing that he'd followed her, was standing in the doorway. 'It's beautiful, Ben. Thank you.' And without actually meaning to, or knowing how it had happened, she flung her arms around his neck and kissed him.

It was a spontaneous, over-in-a-second, thank-you kiss. No one could have mistaken it for anything else. But he'd caught her as she'd flung herself at him. His strong hands were holding her just above the waist, and as she drew back he didn't let her go.

There was a streak of wood ash across his cheek, and she touched it, silky smooth against the stubble of his beard. Laid her hand against his cheek.

There was a stillness about him that seemed to spread to the air around them, and the world, a moment before filled with small noises—a blackbird pinking with annoyance at some disturbance, a car door banging, the steady humming of a lawnmower—was silent.

The only thing she could see was the small fan of lines that radiated from the corner of his eye. Not a smile, but the promise of one. The incredible blue of a gaze that seemed to see, to know everything that she was thinking. No, not thinking, feeling.

Take the balloon ride, Ellie…

The words seemed to come from inside her head, but it was Sean's voice she heard, and her eyes were prickling with tears as she kissed Ben Faulkner again, not impulsively, not an over-in-a-second peck, but slowly, thoughtfully, in a lingering touch of her lips to his.

Someone sighed, it might have been her, and Ben drew her closer, wrapping her in the elemental scents of woodsmoke, clean sweat, hard physical work, deepening the kiss to something that had nothing of the boy-next-door about it, but with something raw and powerful that seeped through every part of her body, firing up damped-down desires, melting her bones, licking over her thighs so that her legs buckled, weak with need.

He caught her close as she dissolved against him, held her so that she could feel his own powerful response, while his other hand gently touched her cheek with dry, garden-roughened fingers, before sliding through her hair. He cradled her head in his palm as she responded to this purely physical raid on her senses, tightening her arms about his neck, opening up to the silk of his tongue, answering him with everything in her that was female, intuitive.

She dropped the trowel as he backed her against the bench, pushed up the T-shirt she was wearing, lowered his mouth to her navel, curling his tongue around the ring she wore there.

'Ben!'

He looked up at her. 'I've wanted to do that since the first moment I saw you.'

'Oh.' She felt a bit giddy. 'Does it, um, live up to expectations?'

'I'll have to try it again to be sure…'

Yes! She was shivery, giddy, first warm, then cold, as his mouth trailed moist kisses over her belly, pushing her T-shirt further as he advanced on her breasts, sucked in a nipple over the thin lace of her bra.

She held in her breath as hot, urgent waves of pure pleasure spread in widening circles from the epicentre of his touch, stoking a hunger, firing a need so strong that it blocked out every thought, everything but this moment, now. Then he touched her, and she was flying, no hot air involved…

'Ben…' She murmured his name.

'Ben.'

There was a sharper echo…

Or maybe not. The voice was not hers, and Ben had stilled. Without a word, he straightened, tugged her T-shirt back to respectability, never once taking his eyes off her.

'Basic Gardening, Lesson One, Ellie,' he said. 'Always lock the potting shed door…' Only then did he turn and say, 'Hello, Natasha.'

CHAPTER TEN

A MOMENT before Ellie had been feeling elemental, powerful, the earth mother being worshipped by man.

All she felt now, in the presence of this tall, slender designer-wrapped snow queen, was pathetic, grubby, easy...

She couldn't bear to look at either of them and, not knowing what to say, where to put her eyes, she seized on the first thing she saw. 'If you'll excuse me, Doc,' she said, picking up the trowel. 'Holes to dig...' maybe she could dig one big enough to hide herself in '... herbs to plant.'

'Ellie, wait.' Ben made to follow her. Natasha stopped him with a touch of her white hand, with its perfectly French polished nails, to his arm.

'Leave the poor girl, Ben.' Then, with a soft laugh, 'Really, you *are* in a bad way if you're knocking off the help in the garden shed. My rescue mission is long overdue.'

Ellie didn't blush. This kind of embarrassment was beyond blushing. She didn't hang around to hear what Ben had to say, either. She needed to take out her feelings on something right now, and innocent soil would feel no pain.

If she kept moving, didn't stop to think, maybe she'd manage to keep one step ahead of it. That was the answer. Grab for life, hold on to it. Keep moving. Don't stop to look back...

She blinked, brushed something from her cheek. Shooed away Millie, who was nibbling at one of the plants with a look of ecstasy on her face. Grabbed a tray of plants.

Lemon balm.

She didn't have to look at the label. As she brushed against a leaf the scent rose, clean and fresh, bringing back that moment in the nursery.

It had been some kind of a turning point for her. The day, so dark and full of bad memories, had turned on that moment, become a day of sunshine and promise...

She dashed away another tear that had escaped. She didn't cry. Wouldn't cry. Tears were useless, pointless, and blinking furiously, biting down on her teeth until she thought they might break, she looked around. She'd planned the layout of the garden, knew where everything would go.

She was halfway through filling the square with the lemon balm when Ben joined her. He didn't say anything. He just picked up a box hedge plant, jabbed an old trowel into the soil with more force than was strictly necessary, scooped out a hole, stuck it in, firmed it down. Repeated the action over and over, completing the edge while she filled in the middle, until the square was complete.

'What's next?' he asked.

'Rosemary.'

They both reached for the same plant. His hand closed over hers. 'I'm sorry...'

'Don't!' They both looked up at the same time. 'It

wasn't your fault, Ben. You've got nothing to be sorry for. It was me.'

'You? What did you do?'

'I threw myself at you. Just as well you stopped at a trowel. If you'd bought the border spade who knows what I'd have done?' She tried to laugh, but the resulting sound was closer to a strangulated hiccup.

He lifted her chin, forced her to face him. 'I wasn't apologising for kissing you, Ellie. Or for anything else I had on my mind. I was apologising for the fact that you were subjected to Natasha's...' He seemed lost for a word. Or maybe he couldn't bring himself to say it.

'She came back expecting to find you pining for her,' Ellie said, rescuing him. 'It must have been something of a shock to find you *in flagrante* in the potting shed.' Especially with the 'help'. Then, because she couldn't help it, had to know, 'Why did she come?'

Even as she asked the question the answer was obvious, even to an idiot like her. Why would she stay away? Let go a man like Ben Faulkner, who was not only her match in looks, in brains, but was kind to small children, animals and even to stupid girls like her?

'I'm sorry. It's none of my business.'

'I turned down a job I was offered last week with UNESCO. To head up a project to catalogue, research ancient languages. She was hoping to change my mind.'

'She flew from New York for that?'

He might be some kind of genius, but if he believed that he was also the dumbest man in the world.

'I had a personal call from the Director-General. Apparently Natasha put my name forward. I imagine she was a touch irritated that I wasn't sufficiently flattered to leap at the chance.'

A touch irritated he hadn't leapt to change his mind, more like.

'I can see why she might be a little put out. It sounds perfect.' Certainly dealt with the question of him trailing in her wake.

'Yes, it does, doesn't it?' He took the plant from her hand, stood up, lifted her to her feet. 'Jetting all over the world, a tax-free salary, prestige coming out of my ears, Natasha's New York loft apartment when we manage to connect for a day or two. She couldn't understand why I'd turn it down.'

'Why did you?'

'I don't get off on that kind of power trip, Ellie.' He looked at the plant he was holding, then at her. 'This is my home. This is where I want to be.'

'She still isn't interested?'

'I didn't offer her the option. In fact I didn't offer her anything other than to call her a taxi. She wanted me to join her for dinner, but when I explained that I had unfinished business with the "help" I finally got through to her.'

'Oh.' Then, 'I was right, then. You can't have it all. I almost feel sorry for her.'

'Only almost? That's harsh, coming from the softest heart in Melchester.'

'That "help" crack is going to take a while…'

He replaced the plant in its tray.

'I think we've done enough here. Do you want to get the hose, give these plants some water, while I put the tools away?' Then, 'I thought we might avoid cooking and give the Italian round the corner a try. If you like Italian food?'

'Love it,' she said, although it probably wouldn't have mattered what he'd suggested. Thai, French,

Japanese, a hot dog from the caravan in the lay-by on the ring road...

She fetched the hose from where it was lying on the path near the bonfire. Tried the trigger mechanism, but nothing happened. 'How does this thing work?'

'It's locked. You have to click the smaller trigger first,' Ben said, passing her with the fork and a rake in one hand, the trowels in the other.

She turned it over for a closer look. 'Like this?'

The water shot out of the spray like a power shower. A freezing cold power shower. Ben made the mistake of laughing, and she turned it on him without a second thought. He caught his breath, too shocked to speak and too hampered by the tools he was carrying to do anything to stop her.

Then he dropped the tools, grabbed the hose and chased her round the garden with it, while she screamed helplessly with laughter until he caught her, brought her down on top of him.

'I surrender,' she shrieked, as he rolled her onto her back and pinned her against the soft grass beneath his dripping body. Then, as she saw the naked desire in his eyes, the laughter died on her lips, and for a moment all they did was look as they caught at their breath.

Then, when she thought she might die if he didn't kiss her, might die if he did, Ben Faulkner's mouth descended with the abrupt, hungry insistence of a starving man who'd found himself unexpectedly offered a feast.

It had been so long. Maybe she'd forgotten the intensity of the feelings, the need, the urgency. Maybe it was just the newness, the strangeness. Or maybe it was none of those things, but something more. Whatever it was, she wanted it. Wanted it all.

Ben finally raised his head, looked at her with eyes that were more black than blue, and despite the icy drenching there was no doubt that his hunger, his need, was as immediate as hers.

'Ellie?' Her name was a soft question, not a demand. He was giving her a choice. A chance to think again. But she didn't want to think…

'As I'm your p-prisoner—' she began. Her voice died on her. This was all new to her. With Sean there had been none of this hesitation, none of this uncertainty, not knowing what the other person was thinking. Even if it was obvious what he was feeling.

There had been no need to flirt, play games, tease. She didn't know how to do this, and Ben wasn't helping. It was like taking a step into the dark when she'd been clinging to a light. Dim, flickering, but safe. She felt as if she'd been running for the last three years. Making a new life. But all she'd been doing was running on the spot. Or maybe around in circles…

And Ben recognized that, needed her to take the step on her own, as he had done. Not to cling to something that was over, gone, but to let it go, turn and walk towards a future that was entirely hers.

She cleared her throat, tried again.

'As I'm your prisoner,' she said thickly, 'it's your duty to get me out of these wet things. Before I catch my death of cold.'

'You appear to be losing your voice. Maybe you should take a hot shower as well?' Then, with a slow smile, 'Under the closest supervision.'

She didn't need hot water when she had his smile to warm her. 'You think I might try to escape?'

'I'm not prepared to take the risk.'

'We'd better use your shower, then. It's, um, bigger.'

'The smaller the shower,' he said, 'the closer the supervision…'

'We could try both.'

The phone was ringing as they reached the house. They ignored it, shedding wet clothes as they made their way through the kitchen, across the hall. The answering machine clicked in as they reached the stairs.

Ben's voice said, 'You've reached Ben Faulkner and Ellie March. Leave a message for either of us after the bleep.'

Startled, Ellie stopped, looked at him. 'When did you record that?'

'Does it matter?'

Yes, weirdly, it did. But before she could work out why, the caller's voice cut in.

'Ellie, it's Becky Thomas. The hospital has just called to say I've got a kidney match. My mother's in California, visiting my sister. Jack's gone to Scotland for a meeting, and he can't get back until tomorrow morning—'

Ben reached over the banister, picked up the phone, said, 'We'll be right there, Becky.'

'Ben…' The word was an unspoken apology, a plea for understanding.

'It's okay, Ellie.' His kiss, long and sweet, was a promise. 'This will keep.'

The weekend was over before life returned to anything like normal. Ellie had stayed with Daisy, leaving her father to spend as much time as possible at the hospital with his wife, and allowing him to leave in the middle of the night in case of emergency.

In response to her appeal Ben had brought her laptop,

so that she could at least get on with her column. Had stayed to share lunch. Spaghetti hoops on toast.

'It's the nearest to Italian we're going to get this week,' she said, as she saw him to the door, then blushed at her boldness.

'Anticipation is half the pleasure, or so they say.'

'It's going to be that good?'

'You are a joy and torment,' he said as he touched her cheek, curling his fingers back into his hand as if even that contact was too much temptation.

'You'll have the wedding to take your mind off it. You will go?'

'I have no choice. But I'll be sure to tell everyone that my girl is too busy being an angel of mercy to come.'

His girl...

She had finished Lady G's column, weaving in the renovation of the herb garden. Then, instead of sending it, she'd written a long letter to Jennifer Cochrane, explaining why she would not be able to continue with it after the initial six-month contract.

It had taken four attempts to get it right.

She was so used to writing 'in character' that it was hard to break out of it, be herself, but she'd finally managed to set down the plain, unvarnished truth. No excuses about family pressures or the children needing her.

It was time to confront reality. The future.

Her future.

It was all there. Who she really was, what she did. How the first column had come to be written just to prove to the rest of the writing group that she could do it. How, instead of owning up straight away, she'd stupidly clung to her character at the interview. How, even though she'd known what she was doing was

wrong, she hadn't been able to turn down such an unexpected opportunity.

Finally, she apologised unreservedly to Mrs
Cochrane and her readers, offering to return the fees
she'd been paid.

She had e-mailed it before she could change her mind
and then, once it was gone, all bridges burned, she'd
begun to search the net for an art college that might be
prepared to take a mature student.

It was another three days before Becky's mother,
who'd jetted back from California as soon as she could
get a flight, recovered sufficiently to take care of Daisy
so that Ellie could go home.

Ben had told her to call him, that he would pick her
up, but she needed a walk, half an hour on her own, so
that she could get everything straight in her head.

Daisy's dad said he'd drop her things off on his way
to the hospital, and she took the long way home, sitting
for a while on a bench by the river.

Clearing the decks with Mrs Cochrane was just the
beginning. She had other people to talk to. Her parents.
Sue. The writing group. But most of all Ben. There were
things he had to know about her, things he had a right
to know before he made any kind of commitment. Even
one as small as dinner for two at an Italian restaurant…

A car was parked in front of the house when she finally
turned in to the drive, and her stomach, already churning
with nerves, sank to her knees. It had been hard enough
to work herself up to this point. Now she was going to
have to wait.

She let herself in the back door and was practically
bowled over by a half-grown dog, leaping from a basket

and hurling itself at her. A mass of soft red fur, long quivering legs, a whirling feathery tail.

'Hey, gorgeous,' she said, wrapping her arms around him in an effort to hold him still. 'What's your name?'

He just grinned.

'Where did you come from?'

No answer to that one, either.

She straightened, expecting to see Ben in the doorway, regarding her with a slightly rueful smile. The door was, unusually, closed. Presumably to keep the dog from bounding through the house and causing total mayhem. 'Okay, boy, back to your basket.' He rolled over, tongue lolling, a stupid look on his face. 'Basket!' she said, in her firmest voice.

He immediately leapt into it, looking pleased with himself, then leapt out again. Right. She eased herself backwards into the hall, pushing him back when he bounded after her so that she could close the door.

Laughing, she headed for Ben's study to let him know she was home, stopped by the hall table, planning to flick through the post, then did a double take as she saw her pastel drawing of the house, beautifully framed, hanging above the table at eye level.

She reached up, touched the frame, incredibly moved. He'd liked it *that* much?

She heard the drawing room door open behind her and turned, heart in mouth.

'Ben...' she began.

'You've got a visitor, Ellie.' His face was blank, giving nothing away, just the way it had been when he'd first come home. When he hadn't smiled. When he'd wanted her gone. 'Jennifer Cochrane?'

It was a question. Like, do you really know this woman? Is what she's saying true?

She covered her mouth with her hand to stop the cry of anguish. She had been going to tell him. Explain. She'd hoped to make him laugh. See the funny side of it. But she'd lost that moment.

Jennifer Cochrane was standing by the window, looking out at the garden, but she turned as Ellie opened the door. Smiled, oblivious of any tension. At least Ben hadn't thrown her out. Hadn't threatened to sue.

She turned back to the garden, waved at the huge oak, barely visible from the French windows and said, 'I imagine that's where Oliver's treehouse was supposed to be?'

She swallowed. 'Yes…' Her mouth opened but no sound emerged. She tried again. 'Yes.'

'Maybe we could build one?'

She knew Ben had followed her, but she didn't dare look at him. 'Build one?' She frowned. 'Why?'

'I explained to Ben that we were hoping to run a special feature in the August edition. A children's party. I thought we'd use some of those sweet play tents your friend makes. Have the children playing old-fashioned games.' *What?* 'Our cookery editor will rustle up some traditional recipes.'

'But there are no children,' Ellie said. 'No husband,' she forced out, aware of Ben at her shoulder. 'Didn't you get my letter? Don't you understand? I wrote to you, explained everything…'

'My dear Gabriella, I may not be young, but I'm not stupid. I realised from the moment you floundered so helplessly over the question of your title that it was no more than a *nom de plume.*'

'You did?'

'I'm as familiar with Debrett's as I am with my own copy. If you'd been the daughter of any peer I would have been able to recite your family tree.'

'Then why—?'

'Why didn't I say something?' She gave a ladylike shrug. 'I thought it would work with our readers, and I was right. They love it. On the other hand, if it had been a disaster I could have used your deception to pull the column and cancel your contract without having to pay you a penny. Publishing is a hard business. You should not have offered to repay me for the three columns I've already published, Gabriella. If I'd been unscrupulous—'

'If!' It was Ben's disgusted response that removed the smile from her perfectly painted lips.

'If I'd been unscrupulous and your column hadn't been such a success, I might have accepted.'

'Take your money. I don't want it!'

For a moment Mrs Cochrane actually looked uncomfortable. But she rallied, said, 'You know, Ellie—I hope I can call you Ellie?—we both deal in fantasy. In your case, the perfect family, living in a charming home with a charming menagerie of pets. That it's fiction doesn't matter. Your writing has enough zap to it to feel like the truth. As I explained to Ben,' she said, 'your column has revitalised the magazine. Readers' letters are pouring in. Ben has shown me the work you're doing on the herb garden. If you're planning to use that we'll run an offer for a herb collection alongside it. The fern offer was a huge success.'

'Oh. Good.'

'I had intended to phone you, make an appointment to look at the garden—assuming it actually existed—to decide whether it would do for the children's party photo-shoot. After I received your e-mail, I decided it might be helpful to call and talk to you. I'm hoping to persuade you to reconsider your decision not to renew your contract.'

'Ellie will need time to think about it, Mrs Cochrane,' Ben said, stepping in before she could answer. 'As I told you, she's been helping out a sick friend for the last few days.'

'Of course. But in the meantime can I go ahead and arrange everything with the photographer? Call the model agency to book the children? Some well-behaved dogs?'

Ellie frowned. 'Models?'

She gave a small shrug. 'Even if the children hadn't been fictitious, there's the privacy issue. We wouldn't have used them.'

'I don't believe this,' Ben said. Then, with a resigned gesture, 'Just let me know in plenty of time so that I can cut the grass.'

'Actually, it might be better left. A lawn full of daisies would be perfect. The children could make daisy chains.'

'I'd better hold off with the weed-and-feed, then.'

'Excellent. And I'll arrange for someone to come and look at the tree, see if we can do something about the treehouse.' She picked up her briefcase, nodded. 'Your next column is due at the end of the week, Ellie.' Then, 'We do have a contract.'

'Yes,' she said. 'I'll make sure you have it in time.'

Ellie left Ben to see her to the door. Heard him say goodbye. The crunch of the wheels on the gravel. Collapsed onto the sofa as she heard him return to confront her.

'You didn't have to do that,' she said, before he could say a word.

'No?'

'No.'

'I just have to perform for you, is that it? Turn on the smile and I'll pull rabbits out of a hat for you. Provide copy. Even restore my mother's garden so that you'll have something to show an agent. Make your name. Help you sell your damned book.'

'No!' How had she ever let it get to this? 'No, Ben. It wasn't like that. I wasn't using you. This all started before you got home. It was the house I used—that inspired me.' There was a copy of the latest issue of *Milady* on the coffee table. Clearly Mrs Cochrane had shown it to him. 'You've seen my drawing?' she said, as if that somehow proved it.

'I've seen it,' he said, his eyes no longer a sun-filled blue, but the colour of wet slate. 'And then?'

She didn't answer.

'You didn't stop at the house, did you, Ellie?'

'No.' The word was little more than a drawn-out breath. 'No, I didn't stop there. You're right. I used you, but it wasn't deliberate. Intentional. You just slipped into the role I'd written. Or maybe it was the other way around. You were the man I wanted him to be. Warm, generous…' She was already in so much trouble that there seemed little point in holding back. 'The kind of man who'd build his kids a treehouse. Who'd take pity on a rabbit.' Then, remembering the half-grown red setter in the kitchen, 'Or a dog.' So much for the hard man who wouldn't give a dumb red setter house room. And, gaining confidence, she went on, 'A man who'd bind up some sorry woman's knee and give her a lift, even when she was causing him all kinds of trouble. Who'd lead a rag-tag group of refugees through the mountains to safety.' She'd had time to waste, had surfed the net, read the reports… 'A hero, Ben. Not some fictional character but a man who lives what he is. Knows himself through and through. You walked into my life and filled the vacancy.'

This time the silence went on so long that she forced herself to look at him.

'Did you really walk into Jennifer Cochrane's office and try to convince her that you were Lady Gabriella March?' he asked.

'I wore my sister's suit,' she said. 'I looked quite… normal. Honestly.' Then, because it was important, 'You weren't in that first column, Ben. Not even in my imagination. I thought you were some doddery old bloke…' She stopped. No point in dwelling on what he'd turned out to be. 'I didn't mean to go through with it. I started writing it as a pastiche, then sort of got carried away. For heaven's sake, who'd have thought someone would buy it? No one wanted my novel, and I was taking that *seriously*.'

She glanced at him, realised that he was trying not to laugh. 'Go ahead,' she said. 'It's okay. Laugh your head off.' The whole thing was clearly risible.

'Hey,' he said, hunkering down beside her. 'Why would I do that?'

'Why, indeed? You're clearly in anything but a laughing mood.' She shook her head. 'It's okay. I don't blame you. The sad thing is that I was going to tell you. Before this…' she made a vague gesture that encompassed them both '…us…went any further.'

'Oh?' And somehow he was on the sofa beside her.

'I've been sitting by the river trying to think of a way to explain what happened.'

'You've done that.'

She shook her head. 'Not just the column, but what happened to my life. How I got to be here.' He took her hand, held it in his, and somehow that made it easier. 'How,' she said, 'if I'd gone back to art when Sean died it would have been admitting that everyone was right.'

'That he was jealous of your talent?'

'He wasn't jealous. He didn't have my choices. He was gifted, wrote the most incredible poetry, but his father had a small business. In the summer before Sean should have left for university his father had a heart attack and he had to stay and take care of things. No university for him. No gap-year. No time to dream of becoming a poet, a novelist. Just the monthly meetings of the local writers' circle. He was their star, the one who had poems published in lofty literary magazines.'

'I'm sorry, Ellie, but I don't understand. Why did you give it up so completely? You could have taught that as easily as English.'

'No!' She yanked her hand away from his. 'He said that, but I couldn't. Art wasn't something I wanted to give to other people. It was something I did for me.' Hand clenched, she struck at her breast. 'It was all about me. It was a totally selfish thing…'

'All or nothing?'

She closed her eyes.

'So you chose nothing and stayed in Melchester to be with him.'

'I couldn't leave him, Ben. He needed me.'

'When he was alive, maybe. But you can't live his life for him, Ellie. You have to be who you are. Let go…'

As she made to repeat the gesture, Ben caught her hand, turned her into his arms, held her while she sobbed for the loss not just of Sean, but of dreams she'd buried so deep that she'd forgotten them.

Held her, gentled her with meaningless sounds, comforted her with his body, his mouth, with the words that she needed.

Later, much later, when her cheek was pressed against his damp shirt, he said, 'So, sweetheart, what are you going to do?'

'About the column?'

'About your life.' Then, '*Your* life. Don't think about anyone else. Just you. Selfish as you like.'

'Make a bonfire,' she hiccuped. 'Burn the novel. Complete my contract with *Milady* magazine—I got the feeling Jennifer Cochrane might sue if I didn't.'

'She's one tough lady. You won't take up her offer?'

She shook her head. 'I'm going to be too busy. I'm going to apply to Melchester Art College, see if they'll take me as a mature student.'

'You don't want to try for London?'

'It would be a tough commute.'

'Commute?'

'I've got an extended family to consider. Millie, Roger, Nigel…'

'And Rufus. Have you met Rufus?'

'I thought you didn't do dumb red setters?'

'He's from a broken home, ended up in the rescue centre. I thought it was time we had a dog and I knew you'd pick him.'

'Thanks.' Then, 'We?'

'I'm your hero, Ellie. You said so.'

'I've got a big mouth.'

'You've got the most perfect mouth I've ever kissed, but if you want London, they'll be safe here with me.'

'Are you telling me to go?'

'I'm telling you to do what you need to do.'

'Setting me free? Like Natasha?'

'No, Ellie. Not like Natasha. If you become the world's greatest artist, I'll trail in your paint-spattered wake to the ends of the earth. Stay here and keep the waifs and strays fed, raise the kids—'

She put her hand over his mouth. 'You said I could be as selfish as I like.'

'I meant it.'

'Then I'm staying here. It's where I want to be. With the waifs. The kids. You.' Then, because that kind of declaration was embarrassing, 'Are you hungry?'

'Starving.'

She suspected he wasn't talking about food, but dragged him to the kitchen anyway, checked the fridge. 'We're a bit Mother Hubbard.' Then, 'What's this?'

'Wedding cake.'

'I'd forgotten all about the wedding,' she said, taking the plate from the fridge, unwrapping the rich fruit cake. 'How was it?'

'Exactly what you'd expect. Lots of silly hats and tears. The bride liked her goat, by the way. Said to tell you it was her absolutely favourite present bar none.'

'Excellent.' Then, 'I bought a silly hat. Nothing but feathers and ribbons. In crushed raspberry.'

'I'm sorry I missed it.'

She shrugged. 'There's always another wedding.'

'Why wait? Let's have our own.'

'Wedding?'

'Isn't it traditional? We get married, ride off into the

sunset in a superannuated sports car. We'll honeymoon in Italy. You'll paint. I'll speak Latin. We'll have an enormous amount of fun making a start on extending the family—who'll have a ready made treehouse—and live happily ever after. You're the expert on romance novels. You must know how it ends.'

'Not too many of the great romances end that way, Ben.'

'Who wants great when we can have this?' he said, putting the plate on the table and taking her in his arms. 'Don't let's wait too long, hmm?' he said, not waiting for her answer but taking up where they'd left off when the phone had rung and interrupted them.

Behind them there was a crash as Rufus took advantage of the fact that they were completely absorbed in what they were doing and finished off the cake.

* * * * *

Mediterranean Nights

Join the guests and crew of Alexandra's Dream, *the newest luxury ship to set sail on the romantic Mediterranean, as they experience the glamorous world of cruising.*

A new Harlequin continuity series begins in June 2007 with FROM RUSSIA, WITH LOVE by Ingrid Weaver

Marina Artamova books a cabin on the luxurious cruise ship Alexandra's Dream, *when she finds out that her orphaned nephew and his adoptive father are aboard. She's determined to be reunited with the boy…but the romantic ambience of the ship and her undeniable attraction to a man she considers her enemy are about to interfere with her quest!*

Turn the page for a sneak preview!

Piraeus, Greece

"THERE SHE IS, Stefan. *Alexandra's Dream.*" David Anderson squatted beside his new son and pointed at the dark blue hull that towered above the pier. The cruise ship was a majestic sight, twelve decks high and as long as a city block. A circle of silver and gold stars, the logo of the Liberty Cruise Line, gleamed from the swept-back smokestack. Like some legendary sea creature born for the water, the ship emanated power from every sleek curve—even at rest it held the promise of motion. "That's going to be our home for the next ten days."

The child beside him remained silent, his cheeks working in and out as he sucked furiously on his thumb. Hair so blond it appeared white ruffled against his forehead in the harbor breeze. The baby-sweet scent unique to the very young mingled with the tang of the sea.

"Ship," David said. "Uh, *parakhod.*"

From beneath his bangs, Stefan looked at the

Alexandra's Dream. Although he didn't release his thumb, the corners of his mouth tightened with the beginning of a smile.

David grinned. That was Stefan's first smile this afternoon, one of only two since they had left the orphanage yesterday. It was probably because of the boat—according to the orphanage staff, the boy loved boats, which was the main reason David had decided to book this cruise. Then again, there was a strong possibility the smile could have been a reaction to David's attempt at pocket-dictionary Russian. Whatever the cause, it was a good start.

The liaison from the adoption agency had claimed that Stefan had been taught some English, but David had yet to see evidence of it. David continued to speak, positive his son would understand his tone even if he couldn't grasp the words. "This is her maiden voyage. Her first trip, just like this is our first trip, and that makes it special." He motioned toward the stage that had been set up on the pier beneath the ship's bow. "That's why everyone's celebrating."

The ship's official christening ceremony had been held the day before and had been a closed affair, with only the cruise-line executives and VIP guests invited, but the stage hadn't yet been disassembled. Banners bearing the blue and white of the Greek flag of the ship's owner, as well as the Liberty circle of stars logo, draped the edges of the platform. In the center, a group of musicians and a dance troupe dressed in traditional white folk costumes performed for the benefit of the *Alexandra's Dream*'s first passengers. Their audience was in a festive mood, snapping their fingers in time to the music while the dancers twirled and wove through their steps.

David bobbed his head to the rhythm of the mandolins. They were playing a folk tune that seemed vaguely familiar, possibly from a movie he'd seen. He hummed a few notes. "Catchy melody, isn't it?"

Stefan turned his gaze on David. His eyes were a striking shade of blue, as cool and pale as a winter horizon and far too solemn for a child not yet five. Still, the smile that hovered at the corners of his mouth persisted. He moved his head with the music, mirroring David's motion.

David gave a silent cheer at the interaction. Hopefully, this cruise would provide countless opportunities for more. "Hey, good for you," he said. "Do you like the music?"

The child's eyes sparked. He withdrew his thumb with a pop. *"Moozika!"*

"Music. Right!" David held out his hand. "Come on, let's go closer so we can watch the dancers."

Stefan grasped David's hand quickly, as if he feared it would be withdrawn. In an instant his budding smile was replaced by a look close to panic.

Did he remember the car accident that had killed his parents? It would be a mercy if he didn't. As far as David knew, Stefan had never spoken of it to anyone. Whatever he had seen had made him run so far from the crash that the police hadn't found him until the next day. The event had traumatized him to the extent that he hadn't uttered a word until his fifth week at the orphanage. Even now he seldom talked.

David sat back on his heels and brushed the hair from

Stefan's forehead. That solemn, too-old gaze locked with his, and for an instant, David felt as if he looked back in time at an image of himself thirty years ago.

He didn't need to speak the same language to understand exactly how this boy felt. He knew what it meant to be alone and powerless among strangers, trying to be brave and tough but wishing with every fiber of his being for a place to belong, to be safe, and most of all for someone to love him....

He knew in his heart he would be a good parent to Stefan. It was why he had never considered halting the adoption process after Ellie had left him. He hadn't balked when he'd learned of the recent claim by Stefan's spinster aunt, either; the absentee relative had shown up too late for her case to be considered. The adoption was meant to be. He and this child already shared a bond that went deeper than paperwork or legalities.

A seagull screeched overhead, making Stefan start and press closer to David.

"That's my boy," David murmured. He swallowed hard, struck by the simple truth of what he had just said.

That's my *boy.*

"I CAN'T BE PATIENT, RUDOLPH. I'm not going to stand by and watch my nephew get ripped from his country and his roots to live on the other side of the world."

Rudolph hissed out a slow breath. "Marina, I don't like the sound of that. What are you planning?"

"I'm going to talk some sense into this American kidnapper."

"No. Absolutely not. No offence, but diplomacy is not your strong suit."

"Diplomacy be damned. Their ship's due to sail at five o'clock."

"Then you wouldn't have an opportunity to speak with him even if his lawyer agreed to a meeting."

"I'll have ten days of opportunities, Rudolph, since I plan to be on board that ship."

* * * * *

Follow Marina and David as they join forces to uncover the reason behind little Stefan's unusual silence, and the secret behind the death of his parents....

Look for From Russia, With Love by Ingrid Weaver in stores June 2007.

HARLEQUIN®

Mediterranean NIGHTS™

Tycoon Elias Stamos is launching his newest luxury cruise ship from his home port in Greece. But someone from his past is eager to expose old secrets and to see the Stamos empire crumble.

Mediterranean Nights
launches in June 2007 with...

FROM RUSSIA, WITH LOVE
by *Ingrid Weaver*

Join the guests and crew of *Alexandra's Dream* as they are drawn into a world of glamour, romance and intrigue in this new 12-book series.

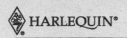

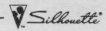
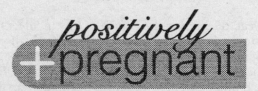

REQUEST YOUR FREE BOOKS!
2 FREE NOVELS PLUS 2
FREE GIFTS!

HARLEQUIN ROMANCE®

From the Heart, For the Heart

HR07